THE DAWN OF UNIONS

THE DAWN OF UNIONS

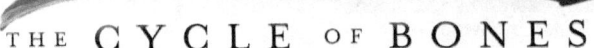

THE CYCLE OF BONES

JP CORWYN

4 Horsemen
Publications, Inc.

The Dawn of Unions
Copyright © 2019, 2023 JP Corwyn, LLC. All rights reserved.
4 Horsemen Publications, Inc.

4 Horsemen
Publications, Inc.

1497 Main St. Suite 169
Dunedin, FL 34698
4horsemenpublications.com
info@4horsemenpublications.com

Cover by Jeff Brown
Typesetting by Niki Tantillo
Edited by Lauren Xena Campbell
Copy Edited by Gwen Hernandez

Library of Congress Control Number: 2023936647

Paperback ISBN-13: 978-1-64450-995-1
Audiobook ISBN-13: 979-8-8232-0154-4
Ebook ISBN-13: 978-1-64450-999-9

As you read *The Dawn of Unions*, Spotify QR Codes can be found throughout with songs from *The Cycle of Bones - Original Soundtrack Vol. 1*. To scan, go to the Spotify app, tap the search tab, then locate the camera icon. This should take you to your camera to scan the QR code.

Below is the first track. Enjoy!

Dedication

People always say "there's never enough time" or "I wish I had more time. I wish I'd said something while I had the chance." I've never really much believed in that. Regardless of whether it's telling somebody that you love them, thanking them for a good turn they did you (whether they knew it or not), letting them know you appreciate them, or that they've done something that either walked up to, or crossed the line with you; there is always time. We just have to remember to take it. For good or ill, people impact your life on a daily basis. Whether they know it or not is largely up to you.

This book, and indeed the entire series, is dedicated to people whom I have never met, and in some cases never will. Never having met them, however, does nothing to diminish the impact they've had on my life. Their words, lives, experiences, and insights have reinforced my own understanding of the world and my place in it, have validated my overarching ideals, have taught me new ways to contextualize things around me, and have humbled me in ways too numerous to list here.

With boundless and grateful thanks to Jocko Willink, Leif Babin and the men of SEAL Team 3, Task Unit Bruiser.

Introduced to me through the proverbial lenses of both Leif and Jocko's writings, and the rather more literal lenses of the cameras which have captured their lessons and their lives for posterity, it is by no means an exaggeration to say that without these men I would be neither who, nor where I am today. Among many other important lessons, they reminded me of a truth I'd always espoused, but had lost sight of (yes, that was both accurate and a blind joke).

It doesn't matter that you're off the path. What matters is that you get on it now.

~JP Corwyn
Clermont, Florida
31 January 2020

TABLE OF CONTENTS

PRELUDE

-I-

A golden hour beneath the sun,
A final foe, the battle won,
When every surface gleamed with light,
We stood in triumph then,

But now, as twilight calls the moon,
And tries to sing an ender's tune,
Surrounded by the eyes of night,
Come stand with me again,

For if this is our final hour,
Then let us greet the Coach Devour,
Surrounded by the eyes of night,
Come stand with me again,
With sword in hand, and spear behind,
Come stand with me again.

He unconsciously slowed his steps so the bag of horseshoes bounced against his hip in time with the rhythms of the song. The leather of the bag he'd slung over his shoulder did an excellent job of muffling the clink jag-jag clink of the iron shoes as they knocked and slid against one another.

You see, Raun? He grinned to himself. *I can play an instrument. Just not one they'd clamor for in a noble's hall.*

He hummed along as he strode toward the group of fellow armsmen singing on the other side of the barn. He wouldn't have time to finish his chore and join them before the song was over, but never mind. There was work to be done. He'd have time to relax once it was sorted. Besides, even if he didn't manage to get to one of the bardic circles before they left tomorrow, he'd have two days in the saddle, a night around the fire, and nearly a week in Westsong to hear Raun perform or sing himself hoarse, arm in arm with the others.

He came to a stop alongside one of the stable boys – though perhaps it would be more appropriate to refer to this one as a stable hand, given his boyhood looked to still be standing some sixteen summers back up the hourglass— half-heartedly brushing down one of the Countess's team of coach horses.

Greggor had spent a year teaching him how to read people by watching them. Though he'd enjoyed the games immensely, the lessons had stopped abruptly on his fourteenth birthday. Those lessons had been given a special place in his memory, alongside those his father had taught him before he'd passed—they were always within easy reach and recall.

Employing them now, however, he saw something that didn't much please him. As near as he could tell, the stable hand was paying far more attention to Raun's song than he was to his work. He was half-humming, half-singing along with the song—*misquoting* the song in a strew of not-quite nonsense words, and wearing a curiously child-like expression on his sharp-featured face.

> *Arounded by the rise of knights,*
> *Come stand ee'up again,*

He might have let it go—might have even done the work for him, if he'd had the time, just to keep things moving along at an even pace. Everyone had moments like that, after all. Given the Countess's departure in the morning, however, there simply wasn't time for the luxury of laziness.

You must always strive to be the bridge, Greggor used to say. *Figure out what your goal is. Once you have, remember it, and make certain you always act in service to that goal. When trying to bring hearts and minds on-side, you can either pass the mug or punch the jaw. It's down to you to figure out which one's best in a given moment.*

"Brought you some shoes," he said. He unslung the bag from over his left shoulder, turned to the right, and took the necessary two strides to lay it atop the nearby wooden table.

"Nay, nay, nay, Kaith! Won't be needing any new shoes today thank'ee very much." His voice was high and somewhat nasally. "No need of new shoes for, oh, 'nother month or so, I sh'think!" He spoke in the inch-thick brogue of the peasantry—a mixture of shortened and unlikely compound words whose first syllables were often swallowed whole in great gusts of rapid speech. The tone used to deliver this cheerful rebuke was full of slightly condescending good humor. The man brushed a hand that looked far too clean for the amount of work his day should be downstream from through the lick of pale brown hair that crowned his head, then went right on humming and half-heartedly brushing the horse's coat.

"No," Kaith's voice was mild. "I thought that too up until this morning."

The stable hand scowled but kept right on humming and sing-songing.

"I made my rounds, spoke to the cartwright, and went with him to inspect the coach. Took a look at horses and tack while I was at it. We found a few nails that needed replacing. He had an order waiting for him, so I picked up fresh ones at old Toby Smithson's forge."

"Nice a'ya." The hand's grunt was as much sarcasm as anything else. "What's it t'do with mi horses?"

Kaith bit back his initial reaction. They most certainly weren't this man's horses, though Kaith knew lots of folk who worked on other people's property for a living and tended to view their business that way.

"It's been a dry season," Kaith answered the man's question as diplomatically as he could, continuing in that same mild, just-passing-the-time tone of voice. "No standing water in the pastures to risk ruining hooves. Most of them should be fine, but two of her Excellency's horses need new shoes on both forelegs. I thought I'd save you the trouble, just as I saved Arlic Cartwright the same, and bring you fresh shoes to settle things before we ride out in the morning." He waited just a moment before finishing, "I've even brought you my tools to help speed up the work."

Everything stopped all at once. Raun ended his song, the four or five other armsmen who had been singing along with him were caught in that magical moment before applause or cheers might break out (the silence that only a truly moving performance can ever really call forth from fighting men), and the stable hand stopped his halfhearted brushing to look greedily over his shoulder at Kaith.

"Y'mean yer Da's old tools? The ones with Sunburst on em?"

Kaith fought against a grin. It wasn't as if his father's blacksmithing tools afforded their wielders some special knowledge or ability to work metal. Nor did his farriering tools serve to calm an otherwise skittish horse while new shoes were applied. Still, a master's tools, regardless of what craft they were tied to, did make the tasks of that craft slightly easier. They often sped the work up by the sheer nature of their efficiency. They also seemed to either inspire or embolden the novice fortunate enough to wield them.

Kaith reckoned it was the tradesman's equivalent of a boy walking around in his father's boots. Using a master's tools just made you feel, well, like a master.

"The very ones," Kaith said, nodding. "If you'd like help, I'm happy to lend a hand, but I suspect you have a better idea of what you're about than I do." In truth, Kaith rather doubted that. Under his father's watchful eye, he'd been making nails and shoes almost since he could first hold a hammer, and he'd been affixing them to a horse's hooves since he was old enough to not be scared of the giant beasts.

Fighting back the urge to smile in triumph, he was inwardly pleased to see he'd gauged the situation rightly. This had been the time to pass the mug, not to punch the jaw.

"Nay, nay, nay, Kaith, I won't be needing help from'ee," he paused, forcing his face to release the scowl it'd begun to wield. "Show me which two horses, and I'll get th'work done."

Kaith nodded, his chin dipping down far enough to be, he hoped, deferential. Raun had begun to voyage on his next performance. Kaith knew it, but couldn't have requested it by name. *Gold and Glory?* Something like that, at any rate.

There's a hold neath the hill,
Where the sons of dead soldiers
Do get drawn down the red ruined road
Where the ghosts of the gone-sires,
Fight and fear they're forgotten
So at glory they grasp, not at gold.

Kaith shook his head to clear it of the imagery, then turned his attention back to the stable hand. He had just opened his mouth to name the horses in question when a young, uneven voice called his name. Surprised and delighted, he turned to look back over his shoulder, his face already splitting into a sunny grin.

Wrapped in the sort of embroidered finery that only the nobility could ever really afford, a youth of fifteen or sixteen who had just about grown into his limbs came striding easily along the length of the stable. His dark brown hair hung in careless bangs, naturally waving off to one side.

"Mi," the stable hand began, voice fighting the tide that dragged it back to its simpering, *I'm a good servant, master, truly,* voice. "Mi'Lord," he managed, bowing.

"Well now," Kaith began in a hearty, chiding tone, "Young master Robis of Wick! What a decided pleasure it is to see you again, my Lord! Tell me how this humble groom can be of assistance to your good self?"

This last sentence came directly on the heels of the one before. Kaith's exaggerated and gently mocking courtesy, caused the younger boy-not-quite-man to smile with genuine good humor, and the stable hand to gasp in shocked incomprehension.

The youth sped up his last few strides and nearly tackled Kaith in a brief, fierce embrace. The sudden movement evinced a deep, uncertain whickering from the mount the stable hand had been half-heartedly attending, and a single stomp for good measure. Robis pulled back from the contact almost as quickly and as fiercely as he'd initiated it, though he gripped both of Kaith's shoulders as he withdrew. He shook Kaith for a moment, eyes wide, mouth still wearing that bright and honest smile.

Kaith laughed at the assault, gripped the youth's shoulders in response, squeezed once, then took a step back: still grinning.

"I hear you and Sir Cedric's men took the prize at the Northern Marches' tournament last month."

"Yes!" Robis' voice performed a few acrobatic leaps between child and manhood in his excitement.

"It's all because of you! You're my secret weapon! Everything—everything you said was right! Nobody'd ever explained it like that before! Not my brother, nor my father, nobody!"

Kaith shook his head, blushing in spite of himself.

"Don't go blaming me for your good fortune, Robis. You did all the—"

"Overthinking? Drowning in my own thoughts? If it hadn't been for you explaining it so plainly, I never would've gotten it straight."

"I hear you were shouting orders and calling cadence the entire time, almost from the Marshall's first call of lay on. I was sad not to have made the trip, but the Countess had other duties for me here in the capital." Valgar had been good enough to give him a full report, and he'd been proud of Robis's obvious improvement.

"I was! And that's my point. Until you told me it was all right to give an order when nobody else was giving one..." His face grew suddenly serious. "That's actually what I wanted to talk to you about. I'm still saying it wrong. I'm doing it right—executing the lessons you taught me—but I can't speak them clearly enough to teach others."

Kaith saw another young man back at the entrance to the stable from whence Robis had come. The two could've been the same age, or perhaps a year separated them. In stark contrast to Robis, however, the lingering newcomer looked absolutely uncertain as to whether or not he should be there.

"Forgive me, may I have your name?"

Kaith turned to see Robis was addressing the room's only other human occupant: the same stable hand he'd been speaking to. For his life, he couldn't remember the man's name. He'd been hoping it would come to him over the course of the conversation, as such things often did.

"Ryko, mi'Lord. Gyfet Ryko, if it please you, sire."

"Guy-fett Rye-ko," Robis repeated, taking care to pronounce each syllable correctly. "Are you a friend of Kaith's, then?"

Ryko took a moment to look sidelong at Kaith, calculating.

In a slow, resigned voice he answered, "Nay, mi Lord. I'm just a humble stable hand. Kaith here was kind enough to bring me some fresh horseshoes to change out before your journey tomorrow and to lend me his father's tools to help me along my way. He's just that sort, is our Kaith. Always happy to lend a hand." He finished this improbable sermon to Kaith's virtue with an almost convincing hunch-shouldered smile.

Robis nodded as if he understood. He took a moment to consider, then seemed to make up his mind.

"Well, if Kaith is willing to lend you his father's tools, he must think highly of you." As Ryko bowed his head and began to show signs of a startlingly convincing blush, Robis continued. "I need to borrow him for a short while. I do hope that's all right."

"Give me just a moment, Robis. I'll meet you and your," he paused before offering a guess, "...cousin?"

Robis' grin made another appearance. He seemed to be doing a lot of that today. "Lamwreigh of Eastshadow," said he. "Sir Cedric's son."

Kaith nodded his head and mouthed an "Ah," before adding, "I won't be a minute."

Robis nodded and turned to walk back the way he'd come. "S'not right," Ryko murmured.

"What isn't?"

"Y'giving advice to boys like that." For a wonder, Ryko sounded earnest, rather than simpering or petulant.

"They're destined for greatness. Both of them are heirs to noble families, both will be knighted, and both will hold the lives of men like'ee and me in their hands."

"What of it?" Kaith was genuinely confused by this suddenly solicitous version of Ryko. "I've not taught him anything new. Just the ebb and flow of melee combat. It's the same thing his father, brother, and other armsmen have taught him since he was old enough to hold a practice sword. I just taught it in a way that made more sense to him ...different words, different examples, same lessons."

"Yer'a groom, aren't you? Ee've no business teaching noble lordlings how'd behave, on or off the field. Certainly, have no business being embraced by them." He shrugged one shoulder, looking away. "If ee'd known 'em since ee's a boy, or a babe'n arms, that might be another thing, but he's from far afield, ain'tee? Wick, was it?" When Kaith nodded a confirmation, Ryko finished his train of thought. "We're n'close, you and I, but I'd not see'ee hanged f'corrupting a noble's get, less o'course ee'd done it. Just..." He trailed off. For a long moment, it looked as if he'd chosen to leave the matter there, but at length, he seemed to decide to press on to the end. "Just keep your distance in public places, is all. Watch yourself, or ye'll wind up swinging f'nothing more than a careless, harmless moment."

Kaith was thunderstruck. In truth, he wasn't certain what surprised him more—the idea that such a simple act of affectionate camaraderie might lead to his death and trouble for Robis, or the fact that, of all people, Ryko was the one offering the warning.

After a moment, Kaith nodded, told the man which two horses needed re-shoeing, and began walking toward Robis and, apparently, the heir to the house of Eastshadow.

-II-

Kaith exited the long stable complex back the way he'd come. He saw the two youths waiting some two or three yards away, leaning against the paddock fence. They were caught in a broad beam of sunlight as it pierced the patchy gray clouds above, and for just a moment, the pair of them looked closer to ten or eleven than the reality of their middle teens.

Robis put an arm around Lamwreigh's shoulders and turned him bodily, as if against his will, so that they were both facing the small remuda of chargers lazily cropping grass beyond the fence. Robis had Lamwreigh by two or perhaps three inches in height, and the pair were at an age where height still mattered. Lamwreigh was a touch broader of chest, however. He also had a shock of raven's-wing black hair crowning his head—a mark of the Venzene heritage carried on his father's side through the past two, perhaps three generations.

Kaith saw Lamwreigh's smile come bursting out from the uncertain expression he'd worn both in the stables and as Robis had turned him. He reckoned it was the horses. The boy's father, Sir Cedric of Eastshadow, was well known to be a fierce combatant on horseback. Kaith suspected his sons were all but bred to the saddle.

"My Lords?" Kaith offered as he neared them. "What can I do to help?"

Robis was still grinning, turning Lamwreigh one more time to face Kaith more directly before dropping the arm from around his shoulder. He took a single half step toward Kaith and reached his right arm out, this time, gripping Kaith's shoulder as he turned back to Lamwreigh.

"Lamwreigh of Eastshadow, Kaith of Thorion—one of the Countess's men. As I told you, I'm no good at explaining it. Not clearly, at any rate. Kaith is the one who explained it to me, and so I thought he'd be the best choice to explain it to you."

Still thinking of what the stable hand had said; Kaith gently extricated himself from under Robis's hand as he stepped forward to bow in deference to Lamwreigh. If Robis noted the brevity of their contact, he seemed to take no offense.

"Robis has been very good to me," Lamwreigh said. Like Robis, his voice hadn't fully finished its transition into manhood, though it seemed to be handling the change with a little less fanfare. His, at least, was a bit smoother in timbre. "I don't know why, but I'm certainly grateful. I'd be grateful for any help you could give, sir."

Kaith straightened, offered a sheepish grin, and shook his head.

"I'm no knight, my Lord, so I think it best we begin there. While I appreciate the honorific, best I be plain with you." Representing oneself as a knight in Thorion County was an offense punishable by, at the least, imprisonment. Depending on what gifts or favors one either received or attempted to receive by virtue of that impersonation, the punishment could well be death.

Lamwreigh blushed, then blanched—a very striking shift in skin color with rather rapid succession.

"You see, Robis?" Lamwreigh shook his head, eyes downcast. "I'm hopeless. It's as if my every meal consisted of little more than boot leather." He chuckled through his mild misery. "...With a bowl of humble pudding for afters..."

His tone suggested he were more darkly amused at himself then outright embarrassed, though judging by his high color; Kaith suspected embarrassment wasn't far below the surface.

Robis shook his head, still grinning. Turning his attention back to Kaith, he spoke anew.

"Lamwreigh was recently betrothed. He finally got to meet his intended at the banquet the night of the tournament."

"I..." Lamwreigh shook his head, then pressed on. "I had no idea how to speak to her," he finally managed. "My feet felt too big and clumsy, my tongue in knots... I was afraid I was going to open my mouth to speak to her and start to drool, trip over myself—break wind or something equally embarrassing!" Whatever embarrassment he'd felt that night, he seemed to be in a good humor about it now, so Kaith reckoned it must've gone alright.

"Fortunately," Robis's tone suggested he was having far too much fun relating the story, "I knew the girl. Alysuun of Southwall—Lady Marcza's younger half-sister."

Kaith nodded, lifting both eyebrows and grinned. If the girl was anything like her elder sister, she would be both fierce and fair.

"And so," said Kaith, "you kindly offered your services to smooth the path, as it were, is that it, Master Robis?"

Robis began to chuckle at Kaith's chiding tone. He nodded and tried on a serious expression that didn't quite fit his face. He seemed incapable of holding onto such a confirmed countenance, however. A breath later; he was chuckling-near-giggling once more. Lamwreigh actually turned and punched him in the arm—an act which turned Robis's chuckle into an outright belly-laugh.

"Well?" Robis might've actually gotten away with sounding wounded if he weren't too busy laughing. "What was I to do? You were just sitting there mooning over her from across the banquet hall, trying desperately not to make eye contact, all the while glaring daggers out of the corner of your eye at any man—even my father mind you—who so much as spoke with her." His laughter faded, though that quicksand smile (which seemed never too far from his face today) made another appearance. "I loudly asked my father whether or not there would be dancing this evening. He thought it an excellent idea, minstrels were called in, and a few minutes after the tables had been cleared away, the evening's dancing had begun."

"Alright, alright, enough," Lamwreigh shoved Robis playfully. It seemed he'd finally reached his limit for stories at his expense today. "We aren't here to mock me. We're here to teach me." He paused, pushing Robis once more. "Something you failed to do, by your own admission." He turned his attention back to the older man. "Kaith. Robis tells me that there is more to command and who gives it during combat than simply the person with the most rank or station. Is that right?"

"That's not..." Kaith paused for a moment, collecting his thoughts, "That's both true and false, my Lord."

"I told you," Robis said. "I can't explain it yet. It makes sense to me, but I can't put it into words that say it plainly." Judging by his tone, Robis seemed more pleased than frustrated at this admission.

"I'll explain it the best I can, my Lords—the same way Greggor and Valgar explained it to me." He looked down for a moment to collect his thoughts. When he saw Lamwreigh's expectant face a moment later, he offered a reassuring smile. "A single stick can easily be broken—that's the individual man on the field. A group of sticks held together is much harder to break—that's the unit, you and your fellows. The hand that brings them and binds them together? That's the leader."

Lamwreigh gave a slow nod.

"So leadership, in its simplest form, is the tie that binds a group together so that it can act together," said Kaith. "One of the most important things you can do as a part of any unit is to keep your mind and actions in lockstep with the person in command. A line only moves as quickly as its slowest man, right? If the line moves with its members each managing a different pace from the person next to them, it isn't really a line. It's a fresh scar waiting to be reopened."

Lamwreigh nodded again. He knew this part already. Like most of the nobility, he'd been trained to fight both alone and in small units from the time he'd been able to lift both shield and wooden sword simultaneously.

"You have to stay together," he said.

"Exactly," Kaith nodded back, offering an encouraging smile. "That means you have to get your mind wrapped around staying on task together. When whomever the commander of your unit happens to be gives an order, you need to be ready to follow it, and you need to make certain that those around you are right in step with you." Seeing Lamwreigh was still with him, Kaith pressed on. "What happens if you see something new on the field, and nobody, not even your commander, is making the call to address it? Are you going to wait for—for example—a flanking unit to come up and strike you and your fellows before you say something?"

Lamwreigh's face showed dawning comprehension: the light beginning to kindle in his eyes.

"No," he laughed, "certainly not. But is it my place to override the commander's plans?"

"Not unless something else is going to override those plans for you, no." Kaith saw Valgar approaching from the castle's grand building. His tall, slender form made him easy to spot even in a sea of other blond heads. He did his best to hurry his lesson along. If Valgar was coming this way, there was a reasonable chance it was Kaith he was looking for. "If you're not passing word to your commander about what you see or hear, you're failing your fellows. If something's coming and there isn't time to pass a question up to whoever is in command, or if there's nobody actively in command, then it's your duty to the rest of your fellows to make the decision, and give the order. If you have a commander still active on the field with you, and he gets cross with you for speaking out of turn, that isn't the time to argue. Explain it to him in as few words as you can while getting your point across. If that doesn't work, let him resume command. Explain to him what you saw—in private, once the battle's ended. If he remains angry, you've learned the type of person you're dealing with. Given your rank and station, you're certainly not going to get flogged over some knight's bad temper. Not saying anything, however, will almost certainly lead to defeat. Saying something, at worst..." He trailed off.

"...Might lead us to survival, and that could lead us to victory." Lamwreigh's face looked thoughtful. His posture and tone suggested that the message had gotten through and that he was already beginning to apply it mentally to previous experiences he'd had or seen.

"Kaith!" Valgar's voice. "You're to come with me. Pardon my Lords," he bowed briefly. "...but the Countess requires the both of us straightaway."

Robis and Lamwreigh simply nodded. As Kaith made a brief bow in their direction, Robis spoke up.

"If we don't get to speak this evening, or on the road to Westsong, we'll come find you around the fire at night, if that suits you?"

Kaith nodded, bade the pair farewell, and fell into step beside Valgar.

He'd hoped that Valgar would explain what it was he was meant to go and do, but the older man was strangely silent as they walked across the cobbles of the courtyard. It wasn't until they'd entered the final hall which led to the throne room that he finally spoke up.

"You and I are to attend her Excellency as she accepts an oath of fealty." He allowed a brief smile to bloom on his face as Kaith nodded his acceptance.

For his part, Kaith was confused as to why he was being called in for a task such as this. Normally this duty would fall to both Valgar and Greggor, after all. Still, if he needed to know more, Valgar would tell him.

As they moved beyond the final doors into the throne room, Kaith noted an aged man in a long white tunic. He was stood a few feet from the Countess as she sat in state. They were speaking, and although their voices were low, they weren't taking pains to be exceptionally quiet. The vaulted ceilings and stone arches made even whispers audible two or three yards away from their source.

Valgar raised a hand to hold them up just inside the main door. Once Kaith had stopped, Valgar nodded off to his right, then clasped his own hands behind his back and spread his feet to shoulders width apart. A moment later and Kaith had mirrored him on his right, as indicated. Silent communication like this was something the pair had worked on for years, almost since Kaith had first joined their number.

"Sir Cedric tells me they've even begun construction on a village and outpost on the north side of the river, your Excellency. According to his scouts, one could charitably consider the rapidity with which they've managed to stand up the hamlet, or thorpe, or however they're officially styling it, as *unnerving*. More colloquially, it's been called *miraculous*."

As the old man spoke, Kaith, at last, recognized him for who he was. Sir Valad—the oldest living knight still in combat service. His voice was rich and sure, carrying with it the sort of natural authority that made it easy to carry out his will and uncomfortable to stand against it.

"I presume the truth is, as is so often the case, somewhere in between those two extremes..." The countess trailed off. This was a long-standing habit—it served to invite others to continue the conversation.

Valad nodded. He paused for a moment, looking down as if collecting his thoughts, then lifted his head again to meet the Countess's eyes.

"The matter seems simple enough, to my mind. There is sorcery at play. That fear, more than any fear over their force of arms, is likely the only reason the vultures here at court haven't sent embassage north. Otherwise, I fear they would actively try and leverage themselves to take Thorion's high seat." This was stated with such a bald, matter-of-fact tone behind it that Valad might have been commenting about falling rain.

"I think *that* goes without saying," the Countess quirked a smile. "After all, reports say that the goblins have increased their forays into the foothills west of the Frost Fangs, there's been no witch-fog rolling in off of the river for nearly a year, and in that time, the Coach Devour hasn't been seen by anyone who could be accounted sober." She paused for a moment, before concluding, "Not since the night of the Long Moon last harvest."

Valad nodded a single time. When he spoke again a moment later, however, the smile that played across his face was plain for everyone in the room to hear.

"And of course, there are those who have come *from* that fledgling northern realm to trade for—and in some cases, outright purchase—slaves in the lower market."

The Countess lifted both slender eyebrows in a look of mild surprise, though her beatific face otherwise bore a bemused expression.

"Very shrewd of you to offer the rights to an otherwise vacant and unused watchtower," Valad continued. "In one stroke, you removed the sudden influx of raw gold coin into Thorion County's economy and prevented bandits from taking over and roosting in a reasonably well-fortified location by placing motivated tenants there. Tenants who are quite used to the expense of mercenary guards, at that. *That* led to you securing trade from that same merchant caravan for, at the very least, another year." He paused, then made a dismissive gesture, before concluding, "Come, Ylspeth... Don't look so surprised. Of what use would I be to you if you were better than me at absolutely everything?"

Her smile was thin but genuine. Of all that served or claimed to serve her and the County throne, only Valad could risk taking such liberty when addressing her. No other could speak to her in such a common and personal manner without fear of reprisal.

"Your base flattery will curry no favor with me *this* day, *Sir* Valad. Of that, you can be certain." Her tone was almost playful, almost sarcastic, and almost genuinely disapproving.

"*Base* flattery? Hardly." He chuckled and shook his head, a whisper of pine song and summer thunder. "I daresay you can still teach half the knights in the County what dunces they truly are with the blade, or what abysmal shots with the bow. Besides, it was you who taught me how to spot such things, *if* you will recall."

"That was some time ago, Sir Valad. I doubt I could even *lift* a sword, let alone wield one, now."

"Fifty years next moonrise, *Countess*." His tone was the audible equivalent of an arched brow. "You began those lessons half a century ago as of next month... I've forgotten neither the date nor the lessons."

She made a gesture of acquiescence, but her look of bemusement was now painted with a thin blush of color that remained stubbornly on her face.

"Tell me, goodly knight —have your reports and scouts told you what name its people call this new realm? Or do most still believe *that region* to be controlled by the mortal servants of the Shivering Song herself?" Her tone made it clear that she, at the least, didn't hold to that opinion.

"Dairy something, Excellency. The Dairy of Khans, I believe." He shrugged, then finished, "Such is the rumor, at any rate. Nothing I would swear to, only what I have heard. It does make a certain amount of sense, given that there have been a great many folk of Shesh heritage spotted north of the river. The leaders of Sheshic nomadic tribes are titled Khans, are they not?"

"They are," said she, "but that is not its name, though you would be forgiven for thinking so. They call it Dereek khn. It's named in the spell tongue, Calyari." She took pains to pronounce the exotic words with care. "*Dair-eek* meaning mountain's and *khonn*, meaning edge. Thus Dereek khn—Mountain's Edge; *that* is how it runs in the Trade Tongue."

He made a gesture of acceptance and let the silence play out.

Further discussion seemed unnecessary. She would make a final decision as to how to interact with their northern neighbors. Her knights would carry that decision forward and do her bidding—most of them, at any rate.

After perhaps thirty seconds, Ylspeth made a gesture with her left hand which beckoned both Valgar and Kaith forward.

Kaith shook himself out of his fervor and did his best not to look thunderstruck by what he'd heard. He wasn't much for political maneuverings and knew very little about gold and the way it worked within larger rooms of power such as this. He'd also never been present for such frank (and frankly high-level) discussions.

After a moment, he and Valgar took up places on either side of the Countess's throne and resumed their stances.

As if at some silent and invisible cue, the aged knight took a step back from the dais upon which the throne sat, centered himself before it, straightened his spine, and spoke in formal tones.

"Your Excellency. I thank you for granting me this audience."

"The Thorion Throne is honored to have you in its presence. What boon would you ask for your many years of excellent service?"

"I have come, your Excellency, to renew my oath of fealty. To kneel today, as I have each year since the first. To know that I have done your bidding, that you are pleased with my service, and, with your blessing, to rise with my mind clean and refocused toward the task of service to the Throne of Thorion County."

The Countess stood, her hair, honey streaked with silver-gray cascading over her shoulders and down her back, and made a gesture to indicate that Valad should proceed.

With no noise save the flutter of his long white tunic, Valad dropped easily to one knee, head bowed, right fist pressed against the lifelike patterns of long grasses which had been deftly rendered upon the throne room's floor.

"Speak your oath, Valad."

There was a long pause before the man obeyed.

"I, Valad of Thorion, Lord of Knell's Stone, do swear upon my life and honor, soul and sword..." When at last he spoke, his voice was steady enough, but his words were carried on a current of obviously strong emotion. "I will teach and train, listen and learn, speak and sponsor, fight and forgive, dream and die in service to the Thorion throne. I will watch and warn, act and accept on the will and word of the keeper of my oath, Ylspeth of Kne—" he cut himself off and amended, "Ylspeth of Thorion: until death take me, the sky falls, or the stars refuse to shine."

The Countess stepped forward, splaying her fingers and laying them atop the short, iron-gray waves of Valad's lowered head. This small ceremony wasn't a matter for pomp or circumstance. Not for this man, at any rate. It had been deeply personal, as if it bore a near-religious significance to him.

When a moment later she began to speak, her voice was no more than a whisper. After a few halting moments, however, it once again wore its customary coat of rich alto tones.

"The Thorion throne hears your words, accepts your oath, and offers you its own: fealty with love, valor with honor, oath-breaking with deadly vengeance." She wiped at her eyes briefly—a very un-Ylspeth action to undertake in public. "Rise, Sir Valad. The Thorion Throne and its protector have need of your service once again."

"With pleasure, Excellency." Valad stood, bowing from the waist.

"Please ensure that we are prepared to depart on schedule, at dawn. Any knight who is not in the column as we leave the northern gate will be left behind. The autumn festival—"

"Will not suffer your Excellency's late arrival." Valad cut her off in a gentle tone. "I have already informed Sirs Anden, Cedric, and Reginald. Giles and Dorean will be with Anden, so that sorts that." He paused, then offered a final bow as he withdrew. "I have you, Excellency. All will be as you command." Ylspeth nodded as the newly re-minted knight backed toward the exit.

In two days' time, they would arrive, fate be kind, at Westsong—one of the few villages that the Countess herself claimed. Three days later, the autumn festival would begin. They would burn wooden carvings of falxes, carve gourds, sing, and dance until the last reveler collapsed in the street, too full of joy to stay awake.

As far as Kaith was aware, it was her favorite time of the year—one of the few events that evoked an absolute and childish joy in her. As Sir Valad departed, the smile on her face made speech unnecessary. She could hardly wait to be on the road at last.

CHAPTER ONE

SPARKS BEFORE STORMWINDS

-I-

*P*eace and prosperity. *They turn us into children again. They let us greet the world with wide-eyed innocence. But the Falx comes for us all, in the end.*

"...And tonight," said she, "The Falx comes to Westsong."

Rising from her perch on the bed, Ylspeth embraced a bitter truth. Setting this village ablaze would evoke a kind of savage, red pleasure within her.

Of course, there would be a reaction from her opposition at court, once word reached them as to what she'd done. What she'd allowed to happen here. They were carrion birds, every one of them. Dressed in finery and falsehood, these effete gossipmongers would gleefully sink their talons into any opportunity if it offered them the chance to conjure or capitalize upon a rival's misfortune, no matter how diaphanous the pretext. They wouldn't be able to resist. They would call her decisions wasteful, a child's tantrum, an old woman's fear. Thorion County's courtiers never could make up their mind whether to think of her as a child or an old woman, which was very convenient for all concerned.

Still, reaction at court be damned. Westsong was her village, they were her peasants, and their fate was in her hands. Hers alone. The only real question was whether or not those same peasants would be allowed to see another morning. That question, she thought, had at last been answered. At least they wouldn't be cold tonight.

Leaving the confines of her bedchamber behind (not that she could recall the last time she'd truly slept), she strode down the hall toward the top of the stairs for what she hoped would be the last time. The heels of her boots made hard, hollow, knocking sounds that stopped the murmured flow of conversation in the rooms below.

"No," she said, "I think this will almost certainly be the last time, come to that." Her tone didn't suggest an epiphany or conclusion, but something rather like a rebuke, as if she were speaking to a much loved, but indolent child. "Whatever falls tonight, I don't expect I'll see another in this place."

She stopped at the top of the oaken staircase and took a moment to comb her fingers through the soft honey and silver of her hair before adjusting the single leather thong she'd chosen to bind it. She spared a last, fleeting thought toward the fit and security of her raiment. She wasn't dressed for court, although she had many lovely things in this place which would have been suitable for such. Instead, she'd chosen dark-hued riding leathers, exquisitely crafted, yet deceptively simple. No, she certainly wasn't arrayed as a noblewoman tonight.

On her left hip, hung where an eating dagger might otherwise have ridden, was a gift from one of her retainers—one of Greggor's personal recommendations, a young man-at-arms named Kaith. The son of a blacksmith, he'd crafted her a long, if plain-looking, hunting knife at some point over the past several days and presented it to her this very afternoon.

The gesture had surprised her, though not because of the craftsmanship or boldness of the gift.

"Excellency, no defense, no defender is perfect," he'd said upon its presentation. "I would rather know that, should the world itself line up against us, you have more than your considerable will and authority to defend yourself with."

It was shocking to hear a warrior of any rank or station, high or low-born, speak of preparation for failure. The norm, after all, was the seemingly endless, self-confident prattling of the career swordsman, crowing about his or her own prowess as the answer to all questions of strategy or safety.

Humility is a virtue that many of my so-called knights would have done well to practice.

A dark smile played itself across her ageless face. Nodding to herself in a satisfied way, Ylspeth squared her shoulders and descended the stairs in even, deliberate strides. It was nearly time.

The sight that met her as she came down gave her a shiver—a species of grim pleasure that bordered on pride. The combination entry and dining hall was filled with activity as all figures great and small knelt, sat, or stood in various states of readiness, packing and preparing, or standing on stolid watch at the enormous bay windows. Each hand and mind, if not every heart, was focused on the task of final preparation for tonight's woeful work, just as she'd ordered. No hand was idle. No one sat listlessly without a task.

Better still, not a single face bore a look of insubordination, mutiny, or hesitation. They were resigned and obedient. It would indeed be her play.

There was work for the very young, and the very old as well. They were often a comfort to one another. Neither group would be appropriate for the delicate work of safely tying knots, taking inventory of small or easily damaged items, or the manufacture of wooden arrows. Rather than being made to sit in the corner like so much forgotten baggage waiting to be called upon, however, they stood in pairs, acting the part of watchmen from the safety of the manor house in which they were all gathered.

Good, she thought, nodding to herself. *Then all of my foes are outside of Westsong.*

Ylspeth took a moment to cast about. As she turned her head, the last spears of sunlight shone through a small western-facing window. Her cheek was brushed with autumn fire as the day's last gleam smote her left eye. The ordinary magic of day's end held for only a moment, but within that moment Greggor approached her.

"Excellency..." Greggor spoke Ylspeth's honorific with respect, yet with an easy familiarity. He stepped toward her, bowed very briefly from the waist, and stood at rough attention with his hands at his sides.

"All appears to be in readiness." Ylspeth concluded this pronouncement with a neutral tone that nonetheless made her words almost a question.

Greggor nodded, his reddish-brown hair falling to either side of his head in waves. "Aye, right enough. While your Excellency was preparing, some of the men even went out to catch our runaways and drag them into the moat's pit." Greggor said this with surprising coolness. "They're sleeping peacefully enough at the moment." Gallows humor was not normally his bailiwick, but it seemed likely that everyone would be more than a trifle off this evening.

"Well, Greggor, if we dally, they'll be burned before we have time to hear them scream." Had her voice ever sounded that cold to her own ears? She didn't think so.

"As you say, Excellency. You'll want to address everyone, I'm certain, afore the fires are lit."

She allowed a smile to bloom, albeit briefly, as she regarded him.

Greggor. Your mind—honestly, even your voice—never fails to comfort me. You, at least, I can always rely on.

"Bring them outside," Ylspeth said. "Call those standing sentry near the bridge, as well. Gather them all before the manor. Let's have done with it."

Greggor nodded, gave another little bow, and turned to the assemblage. He made quick work of motivating everyone toward the exit, save for the watchmen.

The manor's two floors held four southern-facing great windows, two per floor, stretching not quite from floor to ceiling. Greggor and Valgar had recommended teams of two per window—old men and women, each with either a boy or girl of less than nine summers to stand watch with them. She had agreed readily enough. She had her mind focused on how to burn Westsong down with the greatest impact to those who stood between her and the County throne. The shutters had been thrown wide so that they could effectively see out into the village and orchard land beyond. They'd see and hear her address well enough from their positions.

Ylspeth watched them file out, hearing Greggor summon the outliers from their posts. They were obviously frightened, obviously resigned to obey her command, but that, she thought, would not be enough. She had set them upon the road. She needed a way to turn their hearts and wills toward moving along that road. Their obedience and resignation would not see them through what was to come, and that simply wouldn't do.

She'd given many public addresses and was reckoned to be very inspiring, at least according to the gentry. Many tournaments had been won in her name. Many songs and poems sung the praises of her gentility, her beauty, and her ability to spur the hearts of men and not a few women on to greatness. But all of those were in happier hour, in the sunlight, with an air of joy and festivity swaddling them in a light and glamour all their own.

Today should have been such a day. Today should have been for cooking and baking, carving and playing. By now the entire village should have been about to sit down to a banquet, followed by singing, dancing, and drinking. By the first snows, the town would be full of a new crop of spring infants, waiting to greet the world after the snows melted. At sundown, she would have given a rousing speech to extol their year's worth of hard work and exhort them to even greater prosperity in the year to come.

It was easy, she reflected, to inspire people who wanted to be inspired. Tonight's work, however, was darksome. She was, after all, forcing them to destroy what they knew ... in some cases all that they had ever known. Prosperity? There was no prosperity in ending all that you knew—not in any sense a normal person could hold on to.

She watched as the last three or four people in line made their way toward the door. After a moment, she, too, made her way outside.

-II-

She faced south, her eyes walking across the stone bridge which served as the town's only entrance. As her vision widened to take in the scene in front of her, she saw that all the preparations she had ordered had been carried out with due diligence.

She could smell the sour fumes from the oily concoction she'd created. Could see it lathered on all buildings in sight, save the manor itself. The general goods store to the east of the bridge and the constabulary and gathering hall facing it from the west looked as if a giant had vomited upon them, covered as they were in a slick, shiny mixture of dung, thatch, and pitch. The same could be said for the rest of the town's remaining structures, though they were much smaller. Their odd coating faded into the general dim of the onrushing twilight.

Beyond them, the small orchard town was surrounded by a deep, man-made cleft, where the ground had been stripped away. Normally this time of year, as the cold began to set in and the autumn storms turned from rain toward sleet and eventually snow, the moat would be full of debris from falling trees, leaves, and human waste. In the spring, as the snows melted and the creeks and rivers unfroze, there would be swiftly-flowing currents that carried fresh water into the town, and filth away from it. This had been one of the village's chief claims to fame—a small marvel of engineering which kept its citizens healthy and their gardens fertile. Now it was full of wood, thatch, old straw, animal dung, and the sorrowful forms of those once accounted as either their protectors or their neighbors.

Ylspeth was satisfied. The village was ready for burning.

Thirty-five souls stood near at hand, facing her—all that was left of the near seventy that had bided here just days ago. Every eye betrayed fear. Every eye sought hers with exhausted intention. They were looking for their next task and their Lady's will. They were greedy for any activity that would either prevent this sunset from being their last or stave off the inevitable for a few moments more.

Not entirely certain what she was going to say, Ylspeth had just drawn breath to speak when she was interrupted.

"Mi'Lady?" The woman's voice was simultaneously piercing and guttural—music born of a lifetime among both the nobility and the peasantry.

"Lady Marcza?" As the woman stepped forward to the front of the small gathering, Ylspeth realized she wished to approach and nodded. "Please join me."

Marcza's hair (somewhere between chestnut and black) seemed to shimmer as she bowed her head and continued walking toward Ylspeth.

"Countess, the preparations you requested; everything is in readiness, and I trust to your satisfaction." Speaking slightly louder than was strictly necessary, the woman moved herself in such a way as to force Ylspeth to turn with her if she wished not to be rude.

She complied, uncertain as to what exactly was going on.

Was Marcza attempting to get behind her?

Surely not another traitor at this late hour... Ylspeth's thoughts barely had time to bloom as Marcza continued her impromptu report.

"We've gathered up every shield and taken an inventory of what weapons we were able to find or quickly fashion. All treasures worth taking from this place have either been buried appropriately or cataloged and packed for shipping. Several carts have been filled with possession and provision alike, and each have been appropriately hitched to either ox or horse teams. We await your word..."

With that, the Lady Marcza ceased both her words and her walking. She laid her dim-hand along the hilt of her sword, steadying it against her left hip as she bowed from the waist.

Ylspeth listened to this litany with another small surge of grim satisfaction. It wasn't until Marcza ended her report and bowed that she realized what the lady had been attempting to tell her. In a flash, she understood, nodded, and said, "Thank you, my Lady Marcza, for ensuring that my will was carried out." She then turned to the others and, with both hands, gestured them to join Marcza.

Confused, they obeyed.

As they moved, Ylspeth alighted on the place where they had but lately stood, facing crowd and manor house alike.

Turning to face the Countess, the crowd was now forced to drink in the backdrop of the village. They were thus greeted with the same vista of preparation and destruction that they had so assiduously tried to distract themselves from truly seeing.

She caught Marcza's eye and nodded to her. The woman only smiled, offered the briefest of nods, and turned her attention to the bridge and the forest beyond it.

After a moment, Ylspeth spoke in a simple, even voice that carried well in the still air.

"Tonight, Westsong will burn."

Everyone knew this, of course, but the reaction was still both emotional and instantaneous. There was a collective gasp, or perhaps a sigh. Tears stained many faces as the truth, at last, struck them. Inwardly, she nodded. Better by far that she pull the thorn. Best to rip out the unsteady foundation of blissful ignorance and heedless hope. She could build them up anew, but not atop a false foundation.

She allowed the painful moment of realization to spin out but drew them on before they could work themselves into a grieving, wet stupor.

"Sir Robis." Ylspeth made her voice rise, shaping it toward the place where she saw the brown-haired orphan. "Come before me please."

"Countess Ylspeth..." Robis said, stepping to the fore with a nearly comical look of confusion upon his boyish face. "I ... am no knight." His tone as he stammered suggested, *as surely you must know.*

Indeed, she did know. There were no knights here. That was, in fact, the largest part of their problem when it came to defense.

She gave the youth, who couldn't have been more than sixteen, an imperious look before responding to his not-quite-question. He would be the first stone of their new foundation—the stone upon and beside which she would lay all the rest.

"Perhaps you would consider doing as I have commanded if you're done educating me?" Her tone was a calculated one. She was being haughty, clearly, but she made certain to sound only mildly put out of countenance. He had, in fact, played his unknowing role flawlessly thus far.

For his part, his face suddenly suffused with a deep and somehow childlike blush. His black eyes shining, Robis murmured assent and walked the rest of the way forward, bowing with eight feet between them, and then knelt.

"Robis, it is my understanding that it is yourself and the Lady Marcza who organized and carried out my will in this place throughout the day. Is this so?"

"Excellency, the credit belongs to far more than merely the Lady Marcza and myself."

She cut him off. "Yes, I'm certain that there were others that you sent to handle this task or that. Who were your captains then?" She knew very well that everyone here had done their part, and that each of the fighting men and women left in Westsong had put their backs and set their minds toward the tasks at hand with due diligence. It was important that everyone else knew it, as well.

"Your own men-at-arms Greggor and Valgar, my Lady..."

"Lady Marcza, Greggor, Valgar?" She gestured to them each as she called their names, her tone of voice lilting into the unspoken question: *would you come here, please?*

One by one they obliged, bowed, and each knelt in turn beside Robis.

"As Robis was kind enough to point out, he is not a member of the gentry of Thorion County." As Ylspeth spoke, a tiny laugh sparked but sputtered out within the gathered crowd. She thought she might be able to fan that spark into something genuine ... possibly even sustaining.

"My apologies, Countess..." Robis sounded fearful of some punishment yet to come. The apology was genuine and full of rue. To be punished here in this makeshift court for a breach of etiquette just before committing the acts of violence and destruction which were planned for this evening was an absurdity not lost on him—nor anyone else, like as not.

Ylspeth scraped her orator's flint and steel anew with her next words.

"If I might be allowed to continue?" she spoke with calculated gentility and amusement, mixed with a dash of prissy disapproval. The effect was immediate. Longer bursts of amusement, as much nervous energy as genuine mirth, came sputtering out of the crowd, and even from the kneeling figures before her. It died fairly quickly, but it was a clear improvement over the half-hearted chuckling they had managed thus far.

Robis opened his mouth and managed an "I..." before Marcza elbowed him and veritably stage-whispered, "Do shut *up*, Robis." This exchange elicited yet another burst of laughter. Before it could noticeably die away, however, Ylspeth raised her hands to the crowd to quiet them.

"You stayed," her voice was undramatic. Flat, simple, and true. There was no need to embellish. "The brave knights which we once had as our stalwart protectors here are either dead or have fled in an effort to save themselves from what I believe they affectionately referred to as 'Her Excellency's Madness.' Have I got that right, Greggor?" She sounded more amused than angered. Her question to Greggor was almost playful.

"Aye Lady, I believe that is how they fashioned it in their shouted farewells, even as they graced us with the image of their yellow backs fleeing town."

"Well," said she, in answer to the dark looks and murmurs the crowd was now giving, "The good news is, it's quite likely we will end up facing them again. Perhaps even tonight, and undoubtedly with reinforcements walking, riding, or galumphing beside them." This met with grim looks from some, and shocked silence from others, their jaws suddenly hung open. She allowed the silence to play out for three or four seconds before continuing.

"We need skilled men and women to protect us. Moreover, I am the Countess of Thorion. I will have knights to protect my person." She paused only long enough to hear her voice fade into the lowering night sky. "There are those who were once granted that honor who are now proven yellow. They did not have the will or character to stand in service to their oaths. They lack the true courage of their sworn convictions. They put their own desires above the will of their Countess, their own fortunes held above those of the people they were meant to... were *sworn* to guard and protect. Yet I see before me worthy men and women who stayed and stood, who see the coming wave of blood and fire and do – not – flinch." Every eye was upon her. Every heart thundered. "There is a *locked gate* between us and tomorrow. It and those who built it and shut it against us believe that we are trapped. They believe there is *no way* we can escape their clutches. They believe there is *nothing* we can do but sit here and wait and mewl and die."

She paused for a moment, assessing their reactions. They were pale. None of them seemed to blink, but from the smallest child to the oldest man, they stared with hot, hungry hope.

"But forged in fire and blood, we have *a key*." She did her best to meet each person's eyes, albeit briefly. This was the true test. "We will not all survive what is to come. Of that, you can be certain. But if we do our part, if *each* of us does our part, Westsong will live, and we will either open that gate or *tear—it—down!*"

They did not cheer. This was not a speech meant to evoke jubilant shouts of praise and enthusiasm. They did, however—each and every one, as far as she could tell—nod and speak in assent with grim determination. That, in fact, had been the desired effect.

What she said next, however, took most of them off guard, as she had expected. It turned the tiny flame of their new courage into a bonfire of not merely hope, but a rather more tangible sense of greed. She hoped it would serve to drive them on, once their courage began to founder.

"Every one of our brave fighting men and women will kneel before me now and rise a Knight of Thorion. As for the rest of you—I hereby name each and every one of you free men and women." The crowd was full of shocked 'Oh's' where firmly set jaws had but lately been. The Countess's words meant that none of them would ever owe labor on their Lord's land. That they could marry without their Lord's permission, settle unclaimed county land to call their own, plant what they pleased when they pleased on that land, and move around from settlement to settlement throughout the county with impunity. It effectively removed them from the shackles of their station, giving them the same rights and privileges enjoyed by other free-folk, such as small-hold farmers, merchants, and tradesmen.

They were overwhelmed. Some of them looked as if they'd been struck in the head by something heavy. Others embraced one another and wept, or excitedly gibbered about what they would do with their newfound freedom.

Ylspeth was satisfied. It was a beginning. The promise of a new dawn. Now they simply had to survive long enough to truly embrace it.

"Arise Sir Robis, Dame Marcza, Sir Greggor, Sir Valgar..." She spent a far too brief time going to each in turn, separately accepting their oaths of fealty, offering a word of praise, thanks, and encouragement. As each aspirant was summoned to kneel before her, she would attempt to commit their name to memory, though she knew Greggor would undoubtedly have written everyone down on one of his blessed lists.

She bade Sir Greggor stand and act as her herald, having him summon the next batch of armsmen before her. It contained Westsong's own constable, a guardsman from her own retinue, the newly orphaned heir to the house of Eastshadow, and two men she had never intended to extract or accept oaths of fealty from. In truth, she doubted they had the capacity to understand what such an oath would mean.

Yaru and Arafad had been caravan guards when they first rode into Westsong a week ago: escorting additional goods the Throne had purchased especially for the festival. They appeared to be of mixed descent, of the steppe tribes of Eoden and the northern sands of Shesh, and were strange in custom. They were also halting in their imperfect speech and were thus generally mistrusted by nearly everyone in Westsong because of it. She knew this and a good deal more about them, but both of them had impressed the shrewd Greggor as being reliable men who knew little of fear. He had taken pains to urge her to press them into service, as with the others, and so she had agreed, despite her misgivings.

"Kneel," said she.

Haltingly, as if performing an action alien to them, the pair obeyed a moment after the others had knelt in the dust of the manor's yard. She once more spent a far-too-brief moment speaking with each, before moving on to the next in line.

"Arise, Sir Alnik." He of the warm brown eyes. "Arise, Sir Jaran. Sir Lamwreigh of Eastshadow. Your father's death cut me to the bone. When we return to the capital for the proper ceremony, you may rest assured that I will restore your ancestral lands and lordship to you."

Face haunted, eyes shining, Lamwreigh nodded.

Another one barely old enough to shave, let alone be accounted a man. Ylspeth struggled to maintain her countenance of determined encouragement. *Hells, he's barely keeping his mingled rage and misery at bay. If he cannot master himself here and now, how will he manage when the fires are lit?* Inwardly, she marked the heir to the Lands of Eastshadow as likely among the first to die.

She nodded back with what she hoped was a fortifying smile. As she moved to begin the small ceremony anew with Yaru, the words she'd been waiting for came at last from one of the aged watchmen in the upper windows.

"Excellency! The sun is down!"

-III-

Kaith stood leaning in the door frame. The entry to the manor itself came hard on the heels of a short flight of two steps. It wasn't much, but the position gave him the effect of being fully a head taller than the crowd at large. He reached up and rubbed his fingers along the stubble of his chin. The wind gusted up from the south, brushing its dirty fingers through his strawberry blond hair. It carried with it the horrid, mingled perfume of oil, dung, mud, and rot which Kaith had helped mix and apply, as the Countess had ordered. Following her instructions, he'd used it to coat the buildings flanking the bridge. She'd said it would burn even in a rainstorm, and he doubted it not one jot. While it didn't look like rain tonight, the burning buildings were a necessary part of Greggor's plan. He intended to control the shape and size of the battlefield for as long as possible, creating a hellishly dangerous choke point to funnel the enemy to where their fighting men would be waiting.

He watched as Arafad rose, now Sir Arafad. Kaith realized he was wrinkling his nose at the smell, but that it might look more as if he were wrinkling it at the idea of Arafad's fortune. He forced the muscles of his face to relax, which ultimately caused him to sneeze. No one offered him a blessing, however. Why would they? They were all too excited.

While the serfs hadn't been elevated to the gentry, the prospects for their future, presuming that they all survived the road between here and Thorionden, were now brighter than they'd ever been before. If they lived, they were all now free men and women. Socially speaking, it was as if each one had been given a fine black charger to carry them from place to place, task to task, and fortune to fortune. Unshackled for the first time in any of their lives, they laughed and cried, planned and postulated as to what their futures now held. For the first time ever, they honestly didn't know.

Kaith's party hadn't been in Westsong a week yet. They'd ended the two-day journey at sunset three nights ago. When the entourage had arrived for the Countess's annual inspection of her lands and the autumn festival, none of the local peasantry could've imagined such an outcome or such an ill fate for so many.

It was a mad confluence—the kind told around fires and in smoky halls with the wind moaning outside, as if the lady of the Shivering Song herself were just beyond the door, riding within the Coach Devour, looking for wayward souls to feast upon.

Who would tell their tale? They were all *living* it, now, but who would be left to tell it at its end?

Everyone, if I have anything to say about it, he thought. No sooner had the thought come to him, fully flowered, than it was banished by the realization that, yes, he had been that arrogant just now. While it wasn't hopeless, the Countess was, he reckoned, quite right. They certainly wouldn't all see tomorrow.

CHAPTER TWO

OF DUST AND IRON

-I-

It had taken them the requisite two days to cover the distance between Thorionden, the County seat, and Westsong. The trip had gone without serious incident, and by the time they'd gotten horses stabled, carts secured (the unloading of all but the necessary goods would wait until the full light of morning) and eaten a light supper, most of them were ready for the luxury of a proper bed.

By mid-afternoon on that first day, people had begun to notice that the place was extremely quiet. It wasn't until later that somebody finally put their finger on what sound was missing: Birdsong.

That evening, someone spied a crow flying overhead that dropped out of the sky like a stone, with no sense of direction or aim. Westsong's game warden, Milton Forester, and his son went out to investigate just near sunset.

They never returned.

During breakfast on the second day, Forester's wife appealed to the Countess for help. Neither husband nor son had returned from the previous night's investigation. As the bird had fallen within bowshot of the town's bridge, she was more than a bit concerned but was wary of venturing out so near to the tree line alone.

As guests in the house, the breakfast table was often seen as an impromptu and informal council table. Forester's wife had been loath to interrupt the meal of the great folk but had been rightly told that Alnik, the constable, was attending her Excellency this morning. She was, in truth, fortunate to have called while so many were there at table. Surely someone would stand to see to the matter and find her missing kin.

Sir Reginald of Wick was among those seated at the table, along with his youngest son, Robis, who Kaith had been seated across from. At sixteen, Robis might not have fully matured physically, but constant training and an insatiable desire to keep up with both his father and his elder brother had driven him farther down that path than most boys his age, and some men with half again his years. As his voice hadn't broken entirely yet, he sounded soft and tentative most of the time, unless he spoke with true excitement. Then he sounded overeager, or worse still, sickly.

The Countess turned her head to look across the table at the assembled knights, squires, and men-at-arms. Most of them, Kaith noted, paid focused attention to their meals: quail eggs, pale breads, fruit, bacon, and a soft, creamy cheese.

The Countess did not actually respond to the peasant woman's concerns with any sort of visual or verbal acknowledgment, but Kaith was certain he understood his mistress's mind.

When, a moment later, the Countess drew the constable's brown-eyed attention by lifting the first finger of her left hand from the tabletop, effectively stopping him before he could rise to attend the Forester woman, Kaith knew he'd been right.

He'd met Robis's eyes across the table, and was about to suggest the youth and, perhaps, Lamwreigh go investigate together when he'd felt a foot squeeze down on the toes of his left boot.

Based on the angle, the press hadn't come from Robis, but from his father, seated in front of Kaith and to the left. When Robis gave no sign he'd felt anything, Sir Reginald caught Kaith's eye, staring a silent question toward him and offered a brief but sheepish smile. A heartbeat later and Robis's face showed surprise and mild pain.

He'd cleared his throat and spoken to the Countess in as clear a voice as he could muster.

"I," he began, "I will go investigate this, your Excellency, by your leave."

"What an excellent idea!" Sir Reginald said. He had flashed a look of surprise to his son, then turned to the Countess. "Excellency, with your permission, I will ride out with my son. It will give me an opportunity to study him in the field, as it were."

The countess had inclined her head, given a gesture of acquiescence, and returned to her quail eggs and Alnik's halting report on the state of affairs here without a word.

Forester's wife was nearly incoherent with relief and shocked gratitude. Rather than the constable, she had somehow managed a knight and his squire to take on the task of looking for her man and boy. She did her best not to make a fool of herself as she offered a torrent of thanks and exited the manor.

-II-

Thirty minutes later found Kaith stood on the balcony of the guardhouse to the east of the bridge. Valgar was with him. This being their first guard shift here at Westsong, and one of Kaith's first half-dozen in total, Valgar was showing Kaith precisely what it was he wanted the younger man to do.

"One of us will be here at all times," Valgar said. "You want to make certain we have short and longbow at the ready, with a quiver's worth of ammunition for each."

Kaith nodded his understanding, then checked the sight lines.

"You'll not need to worry too much about anything coming from the east or west, though you should keep an ear out, if you take my meaning."

Kaith had just been about to ask. The balcony offered a fantastic view of the bridge and road south, the only way to get into or out of the village, but the view to the east was utterly blocked by the upper floor to which the balcony was attached. There was no place along the parapet that allowed any sort of vantage in that direction. The general store across the road was also two stories tall, blocking much of the westward view. After a moment's contemplation, understanding broke upon Kaith's face, causing Valgar to smile.

"From here we command the road and the bridge..." Kaith said. He paused only for a moment, then pressed on with a nod.

"The moat prevents anyone from ambling into Westsong from the east or west, and both the general store across the road." He knocked on the wall behind him with the back of his left hand.

"And this second story provides nearly flawless cover from any approaching force, or if it came to that, assaulting archer fire from either direction."

Valgar's slightly oversized mouth stretched into a smile of pleasure that was almost comical. "Absolutely right," he said. "I'm sure I don't have to tell you why both sets of archery gear are needed. You know the weapons better than I do."

"How to build and repair them, maybe. You're certainly better at their use than I am," Kaith said. Without pausing to give Valgar an opportunity to argue, Kaith pressed on. "The short bow has nowhere near the range of the long but is perfect if you don't mean to shoot in an arc. All the power in a straight line."

Valgar nodded, his face still split in that slightly oversized but unmistakably sunny grin.

"The longbow obviously provides greater range, but the shots have to arc in order to best make use of that. We can hit them easily enough if there's a *them* to hit, just this side of the tree line if that's too far for the short bow." Kaith paused, considering, then mouthed an '*ah*' before concluding, "But it can also be used for a comparatively silent signal to somebody in the village." He was picturing the need to signal a guard back at the manor house without waking the entire town—something coming on the road perhaps, worth alerting all on-duty guards about, but not waking the whole town over.

Valgar's smile evaporated to be replaced by a look of abject vacuity.

"What? No!" Valgar said. "Longbow's there in case you spot a deer while on duty. If it's out of short bow range, you can fell the thing with a shot from longbow."

Valgar said the word *longbow* as if it was someone's name, dropping the word "the," which would normally have heralded it.

Kaith doubted if the man were even aware that he was doing it. It was a holdover from his first fifteen years of life. He'd grown up in Birchorg a few days ride from the capital. Such rural upbringing meant Valgar hadn't ever altogether lost the peasant patois he'd carried out of his first home. Greggor had outright purchased him from that village's bailiff, but Kaith had never gotten the story in its entirety. Valgar hadn't ever been terribly forthcoming about his past. As easy-going as the man was in all other matters, that had always struck Kaith as strange.

"Hadn't thought of signaling with it, though." Valgar's musing voice brought him back to the moment at hand.

Kaith grinned. He pointed above the lintel where a broad metal sculpture hung. It had been crafted of brass fitted decoratively into iron and made to look like the cup of a rose with its petals unfurled.

"Are we meant to beat that pretty thing when we actually have to sound the alarm?" It was clear from Kaith's tone that he was amused by the idea. The fact that someone would pay to have an alarm klaxon, a large chunk of metal whose sole purpose was to be beaten violently in order to raise an alarm, sculpted and shaped into a work of art worth the value of most villages was an oddment, to be sure. It was the sort of frivolity only a noble would even consider, let alone commission. Still, Kaith could see that the thing was well-crafted, and its creator's decision to unfurl the pedals wide and exaggerate the depth of the cup would shape the sound it made while it was being beaten. He'd learned about how to shape and dissipate sound from his father before he'd passed. A blacksmith who had done his share of work on both weapons and armor, his father had shown him how, in a warrior's helm, sound changed based on the angles of the metal as they related to the ear.

Valgar looked at Kaith, then at the giant rose sculpture, then back at Kaith. His eyes were huge. Tentatively, he reached up with his right hand and knocked on the rose. The soft, resonant *bong* that resulted caused him to recoil, then grin sheepishly as he looked back at Kaith.

"How did you know?" Valgar asked this with a tone of deep respect and obvious wonder.

Kaith shrugged. "The metal, the position, the overall shape, and so on." He wasn't trying to be falsely modest, nor was he trying to belittle the older man. Kaith just knew what he knew. He saw no need to thump his own chest about it.

The wonder left Valgar's face and was replaced with a slow, sly grin. He put a hand on Kaith's shoulder and offered him a nod. "I've come here eleven of the last thirteen years in the Countess' service, and never knew that. Are all smith's sons as bright as new steel, or is it just you?" Valgar laughed.

Kaith returned the grin and then chuckled. "Aye, well we have to do something," he said. "We can't all be born pretty as a maid, like you."

Valgar shoved him playfully but kept his hand prudently on Kaith's shoulder so as not to accidentally send him tumbling off of the balcony.

"By the way, heard some of the knights talking earlier," Kaith said. The grin hadn't left his face, though his voice sounded serious enough. "They asked who the willowy woman in the pretty green dress might be. They noted her this morning as she was heading to the jakes, and were curious as to whether or not she was married."

Valgar looked confused until Kaith reached over and plucked at the other man's green tunic. It hung long, stretching down to midcalf. It was split down the front to allow him to sit easily in the saddle. Unbelted, however, and from behind, it could certainly have been mistaken for a dress in the early morning dimness.

Kaith laughed at the mock-indignance that sprang to Valgar's face. A moment later, he struggled to defend himself from the incoming punches that Valgar rained on him. They were halfhearted, more amused frustration than anything else, though his face was red with embarrassment.

"What are you complaining about? I only told one of them which room was yours, and he's the richest of the lot!" Kaith said.

It was then that they'd heard the screams.

Valgar pulled his dagger from its sheath and began to beat its pommel against the rose, raising the alarm, even as Kaith grabbed up the short-bow and slung its quiver over his head to rest on one shoulder. He knocked an arrow and looked toward where he gauged the screams were coming from.

Squires and men-at-arms came rushing toward the bridge, weapons at the ready. The tattoo of rapid hoofbeats pounded out a hectic rhythm to accompany the scream. It was definitely one scream now. The other had ... ceased.

A moment later, the assembled armsmen saw young Robis thundering toward the bridge, his frame bent low over the neck of his horse, riding for all the world as if death itself dogged his heels, and, yes—screaming.

The men let him pass over the bridge and into the town without a challenge. They closed up rank behind him, facing the orchard land which lay beyond the grasses to the south of town. Nothing moved. Nothing gave chase.

Valgar stopped beating the rose once Robis was over the bridge.

Kaith heard indistinct shouts and recognized the voices of several of the knights. They had obviously come out of the manor house—swords in hand, no doubt—at the sound of the alarm.

Squinting, his eyes following the line made by his knocked arrow, Kaith saw the unmistakable white flank of a horse lying down in the tall grass some hundred yards south of town. It wasn't moving.

Hadn't he seen Robis's father on a horse that color? He wondered if, perhaps, something had spooked Sir Reginald's horse and it had fallen over. If it'd crushed his father, that might explain Robis's fear. If he'd never seen death before, his father being crushed might be enough to run him mad, temporarily at least.

He opened his mouth to say something to that effect to Valgar when the other man spoke up.

"You have the watch," Valgar said. His voice was somber, and a bit clipped. "I'm for Greggor to see what he'd have of us."

Kaith called his name to hold him up. In short order, he told Valgar what he'd seen, and what he suspected. Valgar thanked him, and entered the guardhouse from the balcony, closing the door behind him.

Ten minutes or so passed before the knights came out to the bridge to question their squires and men-at-arms. In hushed tones Kaith couldn't hear clearly, they told their lords what they'd seen. When, some thirty minutes later, Valgar and Greggor came to find him, they told him the strange tale the young lord had recounted. Robis's report had been disconcerting, to say the least. *Speak the truth and spurn the treasure.* Had it not been for witnesses among the armsmen, nobody would've *believed* the tale.

-III-

"Sir Reginald and Robis found the man and boy, right enough," Greggor said, "dead with their throats and stomachs gored." He spoke simply, his voice calm, devoid of emotion. "A wolf lay within arm's reach of the pair. Forester's dagger, his hand still white-knuckled around it, was buried to the hilt in the beast's throat. What had happened seemed clear enough."

Kaith's nod was perfunctory. His desire to go and see Robis—to check on him and offer condolences—was currently at war with his duty to hear and understand to the best of his ability, and to await further orders from Greggor and Valgar. As Greggor continued his tale, Kaith's duty won out, but it was a near thing.

"Sir Reginald had dismounted, walked over to the nearest corpse, that of the boy, and slung it over his shoulder. He'd turned back toward his horse when the boy began to move."

At first, they were overjoyed thinking perhaps they'd arrived in time after all. Those hopes, however, were quickly dashed.

"The boy had struggled, and finally managed to push his way up so that he was seated in Reginald's left arm." Here Greggor paused, his face betraying a mixture of sorrow and disgust.

"According to Robis, Reginald turned his smiling face toward the boy, as if to ask him how he was feeling, but before he could open his mouth, the boy opened his own and buried it in Reginald's gullet."

Greggor's voice grew hollow, but he pressed on in spite of his obvious discomfort. "Robis described the boy's skin as shifting to an unnatural blue. He thinks he saw a mouth full of wolf's teeth, and dark-colored nails at the end of his fingers, but that may just be his horror talking. Sir Reginald's screams had been cut off very suddenly. He collapsed to the ground with the boy still making what Robis hauntingly describes as wet, gnawing sounds at the soft flesh of the old man's throat."

He took a moment to collect himself, cleared his throat in an obvious effort to stave off picking the tale up again, but finally, he seemed to decide that it was best to see it through to the end and have done. "Robis screamed, attempted to move forward, and both Milton and the wolf's bodies leapt to their respective feet, lunging toward him. As Robis spurred his own horse away, he saw Milton lunge toward Reginald. The wolf was running, hells bent for pudding, on his own heels. Both Forester and the wolf disappeared back into the grass before Robis had made it more than a few yards."

"This last is confirmed by some of the armsmen who stood at the bridge after we sounded the alarm," said Valgar. It was like him to share or utterly give away glory or credit for quick thinking, even when he alone was truly responsible. Conversely, he rarely shared the blame when blame was necessary. "Several of them reported seeing a man and a dog, or perhaps a wolf, giving chase on foot, before appearing to trip and fall into the grasslands. They didn't rise again."

"Robis..." Kaith blanched at the grim tale. After a moment, he forced himself to ask what he feared was the obvious question. "Are we to go and investigate?" He wasn't excited at the prospect but knew it needed to be done.

"No," Greggor said. "Sir Cedric will take some of his men-at-arms to accomplish that chore. Depending on what he sees..." Greggor trailed off.

"We'll likely know whether this is a plague or curse." Valgar said. If Greggor minded the younger man finishing his sentence, he gave no sign.

Kaith furrowed his brow. After a moment during which he tried to answer his own question and found that he couldn't, he asked aloud.

"How? Moreover, what's the difference between a plague and a curse, in this context at least?" He wasn't certain if he should feel like a fool for not knowing, but fool or not, the fact remained that he *didn't* know, and, as his father always told him, *silence won't remedy that.*

Greggor and Valgar exchanged a look, but Kaith reckoned the exchange served only to determine which of them would answer the questions. After a moment, Greggor nodded and began to speak.

"There's no way to be utterly sure unless you're the one who brings such an evil down on a place or person. Usually, at least according to what you might call *old wisdom*, a plague requires a wound, usually a bite, from one of the infected. A curse, on the other hand, only requires death in a particular area. In an accursed place, the dead don't stay quiet, no matter how they die." He paused, as he often did, to collect and order his thoughts, then finished his explanation in a more businesslike tone—the efficient administrator once again, despite the grim subject matter.

"If they can find bite or claw marks on the wolf itself, that would be a fairly plain sign. If there were birds in the area, they could kill one and see if it stood back up, but as there aren't any, options are limited."

He paused for just a moment, looking as if he were mulling something over. At length, he seemed to come to a decision, and concluded, "If they can't make a clear case one way or t'other on their own, it's likely they'll take either a corpse or heads for proving the truth of what we face here. A skilled enough alchemist should be able to determine the difference. So..." He stood up from his hunkered position and turned to go. "I'd better start asking around to see if we have such a one here, or if there's one in a nearby village just in case."

"In the meantime," said Valgar, "sharpen the spears, the glaives, and the bill hooks." With a pale resolve, he added: "We'll want weapons that have reach if it comes to fighting."

Kaith tried on a look of grim determination without much success. He'd managed to adopt the look easy enough, but it felt like it was going to suddenly slip from his face at any moment, revealing the truth. He was treading water, emotionally speaking.

Hoping to stave off questions, or worse, coddling sympathy, he'd nodded, gave them both a searching look and then moved off to do precisely as Valgar had commanded.

-IV-

Valgar approached, pulling him out of his reverie. *Sir* Valgar, he amended, was a man only a few years older than him at twenty-eight. His long hair and full beard were a sun-bleached blond. His limbs were long and thin, yet there was good muscle there. He put a hand on Kaith's shoulder, his hazel eyes knowing, and full of mirth.

Kaith gave him a deep, deferential nod and a quick smile before returning his attention to the small ceremony going on beyond the crowd.

He saw Lamwreigh's face as the youth of fifteen attached his spurs. He looked uncertain as to whether or not he wanted to find something to stab, or merely to weep. Kaith understood why.

-V-

Robis's story had been verified by Sir Cedric of Eastshadow. He had found the grim tableau near the edge of the grass-lands without much trouble. Though they'd stayed clear of the fallen Sir Reginald for fear he would awaken with a spark of his old skill, they kept Milton, his son, and the wolf at bay with long spears and lances before removing their heads.

Lamwreigh's father had then undertaken the next grim duty.

He took his youngest son, his second squire (Lamwreigh was technically his first) and their three men-at-arms and rode with all haste to the village of Longwheat. It lay a day to the south by cart, but with fast horses, there was every chance they would make it before sundown. Greggor learned that Longwheat had a skilled apothecary amongst its villagers, and so Sir Cedric had taken the three heads in an unlovely burlap sack to be tested through some arcane rootcraft for signs of plague and disease.

Several families had loaded their wagons and left with the Eastshadow party. They didn't want to remain while their home was under such an evil omen. Fourteen men, women, and children followed Sir Cedric's van to the south. None of them had returned, as of yet.

Kaith had spent an unsuccessful hour trying to speak with and, perhaps, offer some consolation to Robis. Robis would have none of it. He'd simply sat in sullen, shocked silence no matter what Kaith had said or done.

Lamwreigh'd found him, miserable and frustrated at his failures, half an hour later, stalking along the inner bank of the moat. They'd spent some time chatting, commiserating, and speculating before the conversation predictably turned to the hybrid subject of fighting, knighting, and arms.

"My father commanded me to remain behind in Westsong. He wanted me to try and 'make an impression' upon the other squires, the other knights, and perhaps even the Countess."

Lamwreigh ran a hand through his raven's-wing-colored locks—a habit he'd unconsciously picked up from Robis. "He took my baby brother, both to keep him from being under my feet and to ease his obvious and obviously justified fear." The chuckle that followed this was sardonic and utterly without mirth. The subtext was plain enough. *What about my fear?*

Kaith was supposed to be the bridge. Greggor had drilled that into him from almost the beginning. He'd been a free tradesman, a serf, and a professional armsman. Such social mobility was rare, if not unheard of, he knew, and that usually gave him the unique perspective needed to bring people together, or show them things from a different side. This time, however, he'd no idea what to say that would strengthen or comfort the youth before him.

He was spared the trouble of thinking about it over much. The sound of the rose being beaten by the guard of the watch drove out all such long thoughts.

Kaith and Lamwreigh bolted toward the bridge, dimhands bracing and steadying their swords along their hips as they ran.

They skidded to a halt, staring.

The horse that should've born Lamwreigh's younger brother came trotting back over the bridge, its white body covered in flecks of blood and a thin sheen of sweat.

"No..." Lamwreigh breathed. "No, no, no, no, no!" It'd been little more than an hour since they'd left for Longwheat. Twenty souls between Sir Cedric's party and the refugees had ridden out to find either answers or a place to weather the storm. Now it was unclear if any had survived at all, let alone made it safely to the apothecary's village.

-VI-

That had been yesterday. Lamwreigh had held up well. He'd spent the rest of the day and half the night with a practice sword in hand, striking the pell. Kaith more than understood. Leagues from home, no close kith or kin near at hand to comfort him... Lamwreigh hadn't had any time to grieve, nor to put either his heart or mind in order.

Every man and most boys are certain they know how they'd react in a given situation. More often than not, they're sure they could kill if they had to, certain they'd be strong in the face of horror and loss. The truth was, those thoughts proved to be so much chest thumping and blustered air as often, if not more often, than they rang true. In the ordinary course of things, there was no guarantee of ever having the opportunity to find out whether those assertions were so much meaningless dust, or were half-buried truths, like iron ore, waiting for fire to shape it and prove its strength. Tonight, in the village of Westsong, the ordinary course of things no longer appeared to hold any sway.

Before the Countess's announcement and the excited hope that it brought, every face had been resigned, every eye full of purpose. It was easy not to be afraid of the dark when the sun was shining. Now that the night had fallen, however, Kaith found himself wondering whether or not their resolve would hold. When faced with the ugly truth of what they were about to undertake, would that resolve proved to be dust or iron? Speak the truth and spurn the treasure—it wasn't simply their resolve he was worried about, nor was it Lamwreigh's. Given what lay before them, he was almost as worried about his own.

CHAPTER THREE

OF SILVER AND BLOOD

-I-

Kaith watched as the Countess fought against the instinct to rush through the already-shortened ceremony. She accepted oaths of fealty at a determinedly measured pace, even as the lowering night sky was swiftly drained of its splendor and warmth.

Next came Barnic, Jastar, Aethan, Raegus, and Gordan—all from Knell's Stone, squires and grooms of Sir Valad's household. That worthy knight had been their third casualty. His death had been a devastating blow to the Countess's remaining force of men.

Kaith had expected the news of his loss to unman her entirely, given what he and Valgar had seen in the throne room. Strangely, she had taken the news in cold, stoic stride, only commanding that his sword be brought to her before his body was wrapped for burning. It was clear that she'd been affected by his death, and deeply, but her resolve and acceptance had been too unnerving to have seemed entirely natural.

Valad's end had not come during a siege, or raid, or any other form of normal attack. He died in single, and what according to tradition was somehow considered *honorable*, combat before dawn yesterday morning.

His opponent (or perhaps it would be more accurate to call him his executioner) had been Sir Anden—a man twice his size, half his age, and as supremely disinterested in what others thought of him, as most common mousers were...

-II-

Kaith had only recently left the warm comfort of his bed. He'd stood in the jakes, having just finished his necessary. He was suddenly aware of a noise. He'd been hearing it for some time actually, and it simply hadn't registered. It was the muted jingle of armor coupled with the sound of horse's hooves walking slowly from around the west side of the manor house, toward the bridge.

He'd frozen midway through the act of tightening his belt, listening.

Valad, Kaith knew, stood a watch with his men. They were all mounted upon or stood by their horses near the bridge. He'd heard a booming voice which was instantly recognizable as Sir Anden's. Initially, he seemed encouraged, thinking that Valad would be eager to flee with him.

"Great minds, Sir Valad. Thou and I are too wise to simply await death when there is a window, are we not?" Anden's voice was full of false good humor, as if he and Valad were in on some private jest.

Valad turned his horse so that he might face the younger man.

"Of what window do you speak, Sir?" came Valad's dry reply. "And where, if I may ask, are you three brave knights bound? For my watch will last for an hour yet, and in any case, three worthy knights and their collective armsmen seems to me a wasted watch by day when all of Westsong is awake."

"Come now," Anden said. "Surely you see that we cannot stay here in this curséd place." The upward lilt at the end of this assessment made his words almost a question. "We must ride in haste while daylight lasts, cover as much ground as we can."

Valad sat silently in his saddle for a long moment, allowing the predawn breeze to ruffle his hair. The moon gave his normally iron-gray waves a salt-and-silver cast. It made him appear somehow otherworldly—as if an out-rider from the vanguard of the Coach Devour had, at last, revealed himself. At length, he spoke anew. "And where, might I inquire, are we to ride in such haste?" His speech was halting, allowing each section of his question to eke out slowly and deliberately. "Surely you would not abandon the Countess to weather this storm alone?"

Anden's face darkened. He sounded affronted, as if he'd been caught by an unkind word from an unexpected quarter. He pressed on, valiant to the last, but it was clear from his falling tone that he no longer expected to win the older knight to his cause. "We must ride for reinforcements!" He was blustering now. "How else are we to defeat the evil that plagues these lands?"

"And what does the Countess say with regards to your plan?"

"Her Excellency knows nothing of defense or battle," Sir Giles cut in. His voice was a gout of greedy fire, a bright inferno of rage and entitlement. "She would rather sit idly by, trying to devise some addlepated plan as to how to defeat this curse! The lands of Westsong have obviously been claimed by the Shivering Song or her servants. I expect to catch sight or sound of the Coach Devour at any moment, but does her Excellency make preparation to save those who can be mounted or carted? No! She waits to see how the Falx falls. Her loyal knights and their households are expected to wait so that she can save her precious peasants and serfs. They bleat and her heart bleeds ... much as yours, old man."

"Peace, Sir Giles," Sir Dorian mock-simpered as he lay a hand on the burly knight's bright-arm. "One day, you may be as aged as this good knight. You will remember this day, then, when you two are doddery and venerable—your arm barely able to lift a sword, no longer able to make iron for the forge."

Sirs Anden and Giles laughed uproariously at this, as did the eight men who followed in their train—squires, and grooms, men-at-arms, all.

Sir Valad said nothing, his men holding equally silent. As the laughter died away and it became clear that neither the insults nor the jeers of Anden's cronies would serve to cow Sir Valad or his men, Anden tried one final gambit.

"I shall not waste another minute discussing this matter with you, Sir. Either stand aside or be moved." His voice was full of a childish, bullying greed that Kaith didn't much care for.

Supremely unconcerned, Valad asked, "Do you mean to challenge me to single combat, Sir?"

Delighted, Anden said, "I do, old man ... for talk sours, and my sword begs my hand!" Then he dismounted.

Kaith had exited the jakes in time to witness this byplay in its entirety. At the call for single combat, he'd wasted no time moving to the rack of long spears which lay to the west side of the manor house's great door and plucked one up.

Anden's combined force had nearly doubled that of Sir Valad—eleven men to six, and Kaith had thought to do something to even those odds somewhat.

One more spear might not matter, but... As the aggressive Sir Anden and his men currently had their backs to Kaith, he'd thought he could do some damage if it came to that.

"Make the circle!" Anden said. His voice held not just a note, but a veritable symphony of savage glee.

"If nothing else will wake you up to your sworn duty..." Valad dismounted in a single, practiced motion, drew his sword, and walked straight into the forming circle, never so much as slowing his pace.

All but one of his men (Kaith thought it was Jastar, but couldn't be sure) dismounted. This last man, without being asked, led his horse, and those of his fellows, away. The rest joined the circle.

A moment later, having seen to all horses, the final man dismounted and joined the others, completing the ring. It stretched across the bridge road. From the outside, its thirty-foot diameter seemed large, but on the inside, it was a tightrope, a seemingly ever-shrinking cage where the faint of heart faced ignominy at tournament and death during duels.

"To the death, old man?" Anden spoke with naked hope.

"A childish, mewling tantrum. If you've decided that only death will shut your milk-swilling mouth..." Valad nodded. "So be it."

With a growl, Anden charged. The swords of the two knights were little more than sparks from where they connected within the blur of movement.

They bore no shields. Anden wielded an oversized bastard sword, Valad a curiously thick, shorter, more tapered blade that seemed to take the finest qualities of both broad and longsword into its makeup. Both weapons had been custom-made, Kaith was certain. Many knights commissioned such weapons once they had earned glory or renown in tournaments or on campaigns, as both of these men had.

The duel was very nearly the literal representation of the age-old debate between skill and power. For a moment, it looked as if skill and experience were going to carry the day. A younger man, full of strength and confidence, Anden rained blow after blow down upon the older man. Valad bore this patiently. He parried and redirected most blows using an aggressive, reactive defense, and outright endured others using harder, less fluid blocks. Valad was proving a maddeningly difficult opponent for Anden, who spat and cursed with every new attack thwarted—but he certainly wouldn't be able to continue at such a pace indefinitely.

At length, Valad seized the combat tempo and took the initiative away from Anden. His block forced Anden's sword upward, allowing him to step in underneath the larger man's strike and come up between Anden's extended arms. The end result of this was that Valad had the edge of his sword at Anden's throat, and Anden looked as if he were attempting to embrace the older man.

"Yield," said Valad, his voice betraying only a hint of heavy breath. "Words in haste need not make wounds that fester. My ego is not so mountainous that I would see us lose a skilled sword-arm out of hand. Come. Yield and I will grant you parole."

Anden released his sword to his left hand, which was not his bright-hand, Kaith knew. At first, it looked as if the matter was to be settled without any bloodshed after all, but before the moment could stretch out toward that bloodless conclusion, it snapped like a pine knot exploding in a bonfire, becoming ephemeral.

Anden raised his head, looking down his nose at the old man, his eyes flicking to his left, toward his sword. At the same moment, he brought his mailed fist to bear against the place where the hinge of the jaw rested along the left side of Valad's head. This was a dishonorable, but not illegal, blow in a duel.

The old man staggered to the side, not quite dropping his own sword. Anden wasted no time pressing his advantage, bringing both hands to bear on his sword hilt, and in three quick strokes, the fight was over.

Anden's final blow gouged a jagged line from Valad's throat diagonally across the right side of his breastplate. It had been delivered with such force behind it that it took Anden two tries to extricate his sword from his foe's armor.

Sir Valad lay bleeding at his feet, and a cheer went up from the majority of the small crowd. Wasting no time, Sirs Giles and Dorian rushed their men to their mounts.

Kaith rushed forward, enraged. He managed to trip Anden with the haft of his borrowed spear, but Sir Giles caught his captain's arm and kept him from overbalancing.

Sir Giles knocked Kaith asprawl by spurring his horse to ram into Kaith's chest.

With a glare that could turn falling snow into summer steam, Anden allowed himself to be led toward his horse and boosted into the saddle. Sir Valad's men drew their swords and tried to rush at the fleeing armsmen, but managed only a few ineffectual strikes as they rode, hells-bent and likely hells-bound for their desertion.

Anden continued to glare over his shoulder at Kaith as his van thundered over the stone bridge and disappeared beneath the shadow of the tree line.

-III-

Kaith cocked his head to the side, coming back from the realm of memory as if he'd heard something. He'd thought, just for a moment, he'd caught a jangle of toneless, tuneless laughter that sounded too far and wee to have come from anyone here. It was gone just as quickly as it'd come—if, in fact, it hadn't simply been his imagination.

He noted a cloud of bats moving against the dim sky, out on their nightly hunting expedition somewhere to the southeast. It comforted him a little. Seeing animals move— even across the star-strewn distance—suggested that they might still be safe.

"Are you ready, then?" Valgar's mouth curled up into a broad smile.

Kaith nodded, offering a dry, "I suppose. The buildings will burn right enough, and if her Excellency is correct— she tries to make a habit of that, we both know—the moat and the refuse inside should do the same, and for a good long while. As long as she's correct, I think we should be fine. So yes. I suppose I'm ready."

Valgar put his hand alongside Kaith's right cheek, patting it roughly before sliding his hand down to the younger man's shoulder and half-cupping the back of his neck.

Kaith turned his eyes to the right to get a better look at Valgar's face, then looked back at the next group being summoned before the Countess. It would be the last, he knew. Then everyone would be sent to their positions, and they would commence the burning of Westsong.

Hemmet and Raun, both of Southwall, were called forward by the Countess. Kaith was pleased, for he accounted both men as friends. They were followed by Samik, a broad-shouldered wall of muscle who'd only recently taken service in Sir Reginald's retinue. He spoke little, mainly due to his horrid stutter. His mind was sharp enough, but his habit was to communicate almost entirely by gesture.

Edren came next handing his spear off to the newly minted Sir Barnic with a nod of thanks. He had fought beside Lady Marcza's father, Sir Gian, and been the man's final squire before he'd passed last winter.

Again, Kaith was distracted, almost certain he'd heard a jangle of discordant laughter from somewhere in the distance. He shuddered as a horse brayed from the manor house's stable, sounding somehow fearsome and unnatural. It reminded him forcibly of the scene that had greeted him as he'd left the manor house just before dawn that morning.

-IV-

His sleep had been troubled, but that seemed to be the way of things here now. Too much had happened, and in too short a period of time. They'd slept all of three nights in Westsong. The avalanche of horror and outright betrayal had cast an understandably darksome pall over the autumn festival plans. While people could adapt enough to weather such storms, they rarely did so with perfect calm and happiness.

He'd opened the door and exited, headed for the day's work, rather than what he'd longed for—another two hours of sleep. He'd started when Edren had called his name, voice uncharacteristically sharp.

"Kaith! Horseman!"

Kaith ran to the makeshift archery range they'd set up to the east of the manor-house, scooped up a bow and quiver of arrows, and dashed toward the bridge, bypassing the rack of spears some ten feet out of his way in order to save time. He'd whistled briefly at Edren. By the time the other man had spared a glance his way, Kaith had already slung the quiver and bow across his back and now held both hands out and up toward him.

Edren stood some fifteen feet above Kaith on the balcony of the guardhouse. Nodding, he'd tossed down a long spear. The nine-foot haft made an easy target, and Kaith caught and readied it in a single smooth motion. Moving to the west side of the road, he laid his spear against the wall of the general store, drew his bow, and nocked an arrow, waiting. He had a melee weapon—an anti-cavalry weapon at that—near to hand, should he need one. For now, it would be ranged combat, if combat were called for.

Four horses came on at a walk from beneath the gloomy, predawn canopy of the apple and pear trees. Their riders were instantly recognizable. Sir Cedric and three of his men-at-arms rode a diamond formation, with Cedric's young son set before him in the saddle. As the riders came to a stop just before the bridge on the orchard side, Kaith gave a glad cry, redirecting his bow so that it pointed downward at his feet.

Edren's voice was a whipcrack. "Raise your bow! Are you blind?"

Kaith was astonished and dismayed, but he did as he'd been bidden. After a moment, his eyes finally stopped seeing what they'd wanted to see, and he at last recognized what Edren had caught from the first.

What he'd initially mistaken for light glinting off the eyes of the new arrivals, he now saw plain—a malevolent inner glow that caused gooseflesh to rise along his arms. Their skin, too, shone a preternatural combination of star-shot blue and liquid shadow that seemed to writhe and dance beneath the light of the half-veiled moon. The horses were not merely covered in patterns of shadow in the chancy moonlight. Rather, they showed the ragged, weeping wounds which had clearly caused their deaths. They weren't breathing but were unnaturally still, like gruesome statues in the garden of the damned.

"I know you..." came Sir Cedric's voice, ragged and raw. "You served the Countess, archer, and you on high..."

"You speak true, Sir Cedric, and your memory is sharp. I am Squire to Sir Gian of Southwall. What business do you have here?" Edren's tone was calm enough, but the hostility he bore Sir Cedric and his gruesome retinue was impossible to miss.

"Your death," Sir Cedric said.

His tone was utterly without threat, but he spoke with a finality and simplicity that caused the hair on the back of Kaith's neck to stand up, joining the gooseflesh on his arms.

"You are, Sir Cedric, welcome to try, but whilst there are only the two of us on watch, I would call the entire town with a single act long before any of your men, or you yourself, could enter this house and climb to my balcony. Even if you killed young Kaith and took his bow, it would not avail you. I would have every hand raised against you, and while you would kill many, I have no doubt, our forces outnumber yours by a fair bit. The town would survive."

Edren spoke simple truths. Those truths, however, had sent Kaith's mind spinning. He was struck by a flash of sudden, terrible realization. He had made himself a target by standing on the ground with archery gear. If it came to a fight, he would almost certainly be dead before Edren had struck the rose a second time.

Sir Cedric nodded amiably enough and opened his mouth to speak, when the small boy of ten who sat before him in the saddle looked up, leaning his head back against his father's mail-clad chest. He spoke in a sweet, childish treble.

"Father? Does he really—do they really hold the Lord of Eastshadow so cheaply? Can I show them? Please?"

Sir Cedric smiled indulgently and ran his fingers through the boy's hair, tousling it. He nodded once, twice, then looked down into the boy's pale face.

"I believe he does, my son. Go on, then. Draw for these brave men a bitter draught of anticipation, ere we depart."

The three armsmen of his retinue chuckled, as did the boy. A haunting, discordant gibbering, their voices called to mind the monsters that lurked under every child's bed, waiting for the candlelight to fade.

"We want no trouble with you, Sir Cedric, and wish only that you and yours be on your way." Edren tried in vain to gain this grim entourage's attention, and was roundly ignored for his trouble. The black-haired boy—Kaith had forgotten his name, if he'd ever known it—bowed his head for just a moment, then slowly raised it to look directly at Kaith. All at once, Kaith heard movement off to his left, then his right from across the bridge. Men, women, children, and beasts (four dogs, two wolves, and a white warhorse, that Kaith could see) stood up out of the grass in a wide swath to either side of bridge and boy. It spanned hundreds of feet in either direction at what appeared to be its outermost limit. This dusky parade ambled its way toward them wearing faces that had ridden away from town in Sir Cedric's train, not two days before.

Kaith opened his mouth to scream, or at least to give some cry of warning to the sleeping townspeople, but he had no voice. Chill fingers strode up his spine—phantoms of fear, rather than a physical presence.

He drew in breath again, determined to give warning when suddenly the sound of struck metal peeled out like a bell: the alarm. Somewhere above him and to his left, Edren—blessed Edren—had found the fortitude and will to beat the claxon with authority and abandon.

Doors burst open, and men rushed toward the sound, drawing weapons and trying to tighten belts as they moved. No sooner had bodies run their course and stood beside Kaith, issuing curses of confusion and fear, than the mounted party turned, easy as you please, and walked back into the last black shadows of the predawn forest. He could hear their laughter—that jangle of tuneless, discordant gibbering that froze the blood, and called all-to-familiar horror to awaken in the unattended corners of the mind.

No sooner had the quartet of horses disappeared into the darkness than came the collective sound of heavy things falling against the grass. Kaith saw each and every corpse that had come loping toward the town fall as if they'd been puppets with their strings cut. Each in turn disappeared from sight, swallowed by the grasses. Westsong was now surrounded. If they attempted to leave, they would meet the same fate as Sir Reginald—who, Kaith noted, had been one of the first corpses to stand up.

-V-

Kaith was once more forced out of his own head and the horror show that bided there, playing and replaying itself during every quiet moment. He felt the pressure of Valgar's hand slip fully to the back of his neck as, to his surprise, the Countess called his own name.

The stiffness left Kaith's spine. His head began to swim.

Foolishly he began to stammer, "No. No, I take care of the weapons and armor... I'm no knight."

Valgar, taking full advantage of Kaith's confused state, began to gently but firmly propel him forward almost as if he were a prisoner. Voice full of barely suppressed mirth, he said, "Yes, yes. Every one of us is well aware. Fortunately, little brother, that's one problem her Excellency's soon to set to right."

Kaith was gently, but firmly, guided down to one knee at the end of the line. The Countess said something, and the assemblage chuckled. His mind could make no sense of it.

He'd been a blacksmith's apprentice until he was ten when his father had died. Then he'd fed himself by working as a laborer on a farm for a year. He'd been either wise or fortunate enough to seize an opportunity, and took service tending horses, weapons, and armor for Greggor. At fourteen, his duties had expanded to encompass Greggor's men, as well. He'd also begun training with Valgar and the rest of her Excellency's armed retinue, but that was in service to creating a failsafe replacement for their melee team at tournament. Injuries happened often in such contests, so it had been prudent to have someone standing by to fill in.

This is madness, he thought. *I'm a tradesman's son. A likely choice for Valgar to squire, certainly... maybe even Robis, but I'm no knight!*

A few moments later, her Excellency was standing directly before him, and all other thoughts fled his mind.

"Kaith," Ylspeth said. "You've served in my personal retinue these past four years. Before that, you spent several years as a groom for my personal guard, serving under Greggor's watchful eye. The Thorion Throne has watched your development for nearly a decade in total. In that time, your worth has become apparent." There were murmurs of approval behind him. "With deliberation, therefore, I call you to service as a Knight of County Thorion, and await your oath of fealty."

For what seemed an interminable amount of time, Kaith had no idea what he might say—what oath he might give. As often happened in times of stress and confusion, the voice of his father came back to him, strong in his mind.

"Choose your words with care and forethought where and whenever you can, for that's best. When that's impossible, it's better to open the gate and let your horses run. They usually know where to go."

His father's voice reached out to him across the years. Kaith smiled in spite of himself, opened his mouth, and did exactly as he'd been bidden.

"I, Kaith of Thorion, do hereby swear to listen and to think, to train and teach, to hear and to be heard, to bolster and to break, to object and to obey, to cover and to kill until the skies are sundered, the stars refused to shine, or death take me."

His words, at first, were met with a shocked silence. It wasn't until later that he would recognize the echoes of Sir Valad's oath in his own. Within that silence, he heard that distant and discordant laughter from somewhere beyond the bridge. He wanted to look up to see if there were something coming up from the south, or some other sign of attack, but he dared not. Resigned, he waited. The Countess laid her fingers on the top of Kaith's head and responded with surprising smoothness.

"The Thorion Throne hears your words, accepts your oath, and offers you its own: fealty with love, valor with honor, oath-breaking with deadly vengeance."

She pulled a silver chain taught between her fingers, its links thick and strong, and lowered it over his head, just as she had with many of the eighteen who came before him. It was a squire's chain, he knew, its steel links polished to a silver sheen. Had it been that of a knight, it would've been gold, not silver.

Fully a dozen of the men who would end this day as knights had begun it as squires. It was common practice for squires to carry at least one spare silver chain, in case one were lost or damaged. Kaith was fairly certain that every silver chain granted anew today had been one of these spares. Such would undoubtedly be replaced with proper chains of station once everyone returned to Thorion's County seat. Its grave weight came to rest against the back of his neck, falling halfway down his chest. The sensation seemed to center him, and grant him perhaps not a sense of peace, but one of calm and surety.

"Arise, Sir Kaith," said she, and then as an aside when Kaith got to his feet, "If you do not feel that you have yet earned this honor, make it your mission to do so. As my first order to you, Sir Kaith, I command you to prove my faith in you as justified." With that, she handed him a squire's matching silver spurs.

Kaith nodded as he accepted them, his face solemn. He was opening his mouth to both thank and assure her, or perhaps himself, that he would do just that. At that moment, however, the watchmen called from the second floor of the manor house:

"Horses!"

-VI-

Orders were shouted before panic could set in, and people rushed as best they could to their assigned stations. There was comfort in having tasks and responsibilities. It was a cold comfort, but it served to stave off the first bite of fear that battle always brought. Kaith moved to run off as well, but Valgar held him back.

"Fasten your spurs." Valgar said.

Kaith looked at him incredulously. "There isn't time for that!"

Valgar's face was solemn and stern. "There is. The others will light the moat, and we aren't facing a massive cavalry charge." Valgar saw Kaith open his mouth to argue further, but he forestalled him. "You'll need their weight to keep your feet to the road, Kaith. I will watch, and see if our need changes, but until then, fasten your spurs."

Kaith nodded, fighting back fear and a nervous grudge toward Valgar for insisting this be done now. He knelt to do as told. When he looked up again, half the town was on fire, and thirty creatures of incalculable malevolence stood or sat astride their stoic mounts on the other side of the bridge, watching the burning.

Valgar handed him a tower shield he'd retrieved from somewhere. Kaith accepted it, nodded his thanks, and the two of them strode across to the meager line which had been erected just north of the bridge, joining its ranks and locking their shields into place on its east side.

CHAPTER FOUR

A FORCED MARCH THROUGH MEMORY

-I-

Silver in the skies,
Silver polished steel,
Wound about my throat
And singing at my heel,
Silver in the air,
Burned, the battlefield,
Silver brushed the rose,
Who summoned me to kneel.

Lamwreigh stood on Kaith's right, his tower shield locked into position. Kaith noted a look flash across the youth's face. He credited its source as relief at no longer having to stand at the line's end.

Valgar now anchored their line to the left. With a dozen mounted fighting men, and more than a score of other assorted men, women, and beasts on foot before them, Kaith was more than glad to have familiar faces there beside him.

"Did I see Sir Anden's men among Cedric's van?" Valgar sounded almost hopeful at the prospect. He'd been livid at Anden's treatment of Sir Valad when Kaith had told him the tale. "Didn't see that simpering pig Giles among them, but..." He trailed off as Greggor barked the order to dress the line.

Fire licked up all around them, but there was enough space between the burning buildings and the line of shields (twelve in all, five pole-weapons behind) to feel the punishing heat without being burned by it directly. Kaith heard the sounds of arrows being loosed from somewhere behind. Yaru and Arafad, doing their level best to thin the herd from the second-story windows of the manor house.

He then heard the shrill tones of Sir Cedric's youngest son.

His childish treble voice seemed incongruously forceful as it overtopped the muscular, rather more primal sound of the burning wood and tar. Kaith couldn't help but recognize the boy's excitement, though he couldn't make out so much as a word above the din.

A moment later there was an enormous gust of wind. Soon after, an unearthly thunderclap rent the night. Though it had been quite clear at sunset, the sky now opened, releasing a deluge of rain. Such a sudden change in the weather absolutely had to be sorcerous in origin. The boy must have been singing blandishments to whatever darksome deity had granted him license to puppeteer the fallen.

Kaith smiled darkly to himself. *I'm afraid water's not going to do much to put those fires out, young master.* The oil that the Countess had ordered mixed with the pitch and dung would have to either burn itself out or be covered by good old-fashioned Skolfish earth.

Kaith heard Sir Cedric yell, "Damn you boy, it isn't working!"

"Fine!" The boy's shouts sounded sulky and sour as if he were overtired.

Kaith started to laugh. He couldn't help himself. The situation was absolutely dire, and yet it sounded like their collective demise was being kept at bay by the megrims of a whining, simpering child allowed to stay up past his bedtime.

He felt Lamwreigh stiffen to his right. All at once, Kaith could no longer find the humor, even gallows humor, in the situation. He hadn't been thinking. Both the boy and his father were also Lamwreigh's kin. Several of the mounted men-at-arms who stood among Sir Cedric's honor guard had been men and boys up the hourglass who had trained with, and in some cases outright *trained,* Lamwreigh. He'd known them all his life. And now they were coming to kill him.

"They aren't your kin, Lamwreigh," Robis said from behind them. He leaned the haft of his glaive atop the place where Kaith and Lamwreigh's shields overlapped and leaned his head forward. "I know they look like the men you know and love, but it's a lie. They're wearing their faces, not carrying their souls." He spoke in the hollow-eyed tones of a grizzled veteran, not a youth in his middle teens.

"But—" Lamwreigh protested.

"But nothing!" Robis cut across him with a sharpness to his voice that Kaith had never heard in a boy his age. "All you have to do is hear them speak, look at their flesh, to know the truth. They are *not your kin.*" Robis emphasized the last three words as if he were throwing darts.

He isn't a boy, though, Kaith thought. *He may have only seen sixteen years, but after what we've seen here?*

"Lanian..." Lamwreigh's voice was choked, little more than a ragged gasp. "I can hear him. My baby brother, much as he hates being called that, still sounds like himself. His voice isn't ragged, his face isn't stained with shadow like the others. Surely he can be saved..."

"Lamwreigh," Robis said. "Listen to him."

"*Sdraliana thoriash inagro misda regna,*" Lanian peeped. His yet-unbroken voice seemed to caress the words, calling to mind the innocence of a child speaking to his favorite pet. Inexplicably, it also called to mind the darker and more disturbing sense of a man crooning to a wet and writhing lover—a supplicant begging for release.

"Has he ever spoken like that before? Have you ever *heard* words like that before?" Robis pressed.

The boy repeated the alien words thrice more, gaining in volume and intensity with each blasphemous decree.

"*Sdraliana thoriash inagro misda regna... Sdraliana thoriash inagro misda regna! Sdraliana thoriash inagro misda regna!*"

Surely such words were blasphemous. *Must* be blasphemous. Hearing them made Kaith's head swim, his belly suddenly full of ice and snow.

"If you have," said Robis, "then I'll be glad to hear it, for they freeze my blood, and understanding their meaning might settle my mind."

Kaith could see Lamwreigh shaking his head. Could hear the sound of leather creaking as the youth gripped his shield and the hilt of his sword more tightly.

Anyone who'd seen such evil, stared it in the all-too-familiar face, and stood to fight against it anyway, Kaith thought, *is certainly worthy of their spurs. Robis and Lamwreigh are no exceptions. And don't they say that knighthood changes a man? Strengthens and forges him anew?*

"They're coming!" Valgar said, nearly sing-songed. "Make ready!"

Kaith could hear the uneven sound of hooves, boots, and something tapping as it ran on the other side of the shield wall, directly toward them. He found this last sound especially disturbing. His rising fear raged against the battle-focus Greggor and Valgar had beaten into him, trying to conjure all manner of answers to the question of what was hurtling toward him.

One image kept emerging on the stage of his fearful mind's eye. Over and over again he saw the wolf that had taken poor Milton Forester. He knew that was impossible, but it was difficult to get the idea out of his head. Alnik had led a group of men out with spears and bill hooks, poking, prodding and dragging the nearby corpses into the moat this afternoon, though they had stayed prudently clear of Robis's father. They still feared he would stand and, retaining the skill at arms he'd been known for in life, would overmatch them. Now each of the so-called "runaways" they'd dragged into that wide, dry moat would be on fire, if not already incinerated, including the wolf found near Forester's body. Still, Kaith's fear refused to accept any other explanation for the strange clicking sound which was even now hurtling directly toward him.

"Lock it up!" Valgar bawled. As one, they echoed the command. As one, the shields tightened up, left edge over neighbor's right, and braced for the impact.

"Here ... they ... come!" Said Valgar. Kaith braced for the impact.

-II-

"Sir Kaith?" It was a boy's voice, hesitant, accompanied by a tentative hand on Kaith's shoulder, shaking it.

Kaith grabbed the wrist out of reflex but stopped himself from squeezing or yanking. His eyes snapped open. He spoke with a voice that hadn't been used in some time.

"I'm awake. What is it?"

The brown-haired boy froze, eyes the size of serving platters.

Kaith released the boy's wrist, reaching his empty hand out to pat him on the shoulder. He flinched away, rather than accepting the touch.

"Relax, boy. You simply pulled me out of a doze. I'm not going to eat you." Kaith did his best to keep the bite of annoyance and frustration out of his voice and didn't entirely succeed.

"Dame Marcza," the boy began but did not finish. It didn't look like he was capable of finishing, as his face was still all eyes.

"You're not going to make me guess, are you?"

Kaith's smile seemed to encourage the boy. He pinked slightly with embarrassment, his face splitting into a reluctant smile of his own.

"Dame Marcza sent me to come and awaken you. She says..." He screwed up his face in an almighty act of concentration, then relaxed as if he'd been trying to, and finally managed to, pass wind. When he spoke, it was in the usual brogue of the peasantry. "She said to tell'ee that we sh'make Ashacre by four of the clock, but she's only g'bout two bells in her before she'll need'ee to spell her."

Kaith nodded after a moment's pause to chew through the messenger's accented words. He took the measure of his own exhaustion and then nodded again. With an effort, he hauled himself to a sitting position. The back of the wagon was not only full of gear, but of awkwardly sprawled, sleeping people. He reached to his right to grab the small retaining wall, then vaulted over the side. He managed to land on his feet, for the wagon wasn't moving terribly fast, but he felt the vibrations shoot up past his knees as he did so.

Standing upright as the wagon finally fully rolled past him, he started walking toward the front of the column. He managed to pat the boy on his shoulder as he passed by the wagon, eliciting an uncertain smile for his effort.

As he walked, he looked up, gauging the time. The sky was a thin, hazy gray. It forcibly reminded him of the smoky air that had permeated Westsong when he'd last seen it. Rather than softening the rising sun, it made its light blinding.

Instead of squinting, he blinked, as Greggor had taught him. Eyes adjusted to light more quickly through rapid blinking than they did through prolonged squinting. He judged the time somewhere near half seven. It might be a bit later, but it certainly wasn't much past the eighth bell yet.

The battle had only lasted perhaps an hour, though time grew funny when swords and spears were in motion. They'd spent another hour tending the wounded and doing their best to stand a nervous watch, in case more of the things revealed themselves. With less than two bells remaining until midnight, they'd moved their column out, following the road to the southeast. By two of the clock, Kaith had been banished to a wagon to take his rest. He protested, but his brothers, sister, and the Countess herself had over-ridden him.

The battle may have only lasted an hour, but while he slept he found he couldn't escape it.

Five or six hours, he thought. *Normally that would've been enough, but riding and watching will almost certainly be more restful than sleep's proven to be.* He shook his head (though whether in negation or simply to clear it, he himself didn't know) and began to move.

In less than a minute, he'd half-staggered his way to the riders at the head of their little column: Marcza and Edren.

"Finally starting to feel it?" Kaith asked. It was Marcza he was specifically addressing, though Edren nodded as well.

"Aye," Marcza said. She smiled cheerfully enough, but her eyes and the heaviness of her voice told a different story. "Starting to, at any rate."

"Well, never fear," Kaith said. "Awake's better than asleep for me. I'd rather fight fatigue than endlessly re-fighting that battle."

Edren grimaced. "I keep thinking..." he began. "We shouldn't have lost so many."

"Edren..." Marcza began. He forestalled her, waving his hand and overriding her.

"You can quote numbers at me all day, Marcza. I knew some of those men. The others came up with them along the tournament circuit from damn near boyhood in some cases."

"A few of them were still boys last night," said she. Her voice was dry. It held none of her normal hang-it-all good humor.

"Mind your damned tongue." Edren's voice was raw and full of a naked emotion that hurt to hear. "By the end of that battle, none of them were boys, and even if they had been, every single one of them *fought* and *died* as befits a knight. I won't have them belittled, nor the fact of their valor forgotten—not by you, not by *anyone* else!"

Marcza bowed her head. After a moment, she spoke, though she didn't meet Edren's eyes.

"You're right, of course. It's just..." Tears began to roll down her face. Her voice was quite steady despite being subdued.

"I know," Edren said finally. His voice had dropped into a low, bitter growl. "We should've... *I* should've done *something.*" After a long moment during which both riders had their heads down, the ears of their horses twitching back nervously, Kaith found his own voice. To his surprise, it was quite steady. Moreover, it carried with it the unhappy wisdom that only abandoned children ever really gain.

"There isn't anything you could have done. Either of you. There isn't anything any of us could have done. When the Falx finally comes for you, no one can help you. The best you can hope for is to make your life—make your death—mean something. In the face of a nearly unimaginable horror, facing down monsters who wore the faces of men and boys they grew up with, the faces of those who *loved* them, every one of them—every one of *us*—stood. Every one of us made certain that our lives, and if it were our time, our deaths, meant something."

Marcza stopped her horse. She dismounted in an awkward, unpracticed manner and handed Kaith the reins. Not a word passed her lips as she completed this chore, though she looked at him through shining eyes. Finally she laid her hand upon his right shoulder, then departed for the wagons in the back for a few hours of likely broken sleep.

Kaith mounted up and rode forward to catch up with Edren. Neither man spoke for the next thirty minutes, but Edren looked at Kaith several times as they rode, then looked away, nodding to himself. Finally, he called Kaith's name. He was going to go wake his replacement and would instruct the man to pull a fresh horse from their train.

Kaith nodded at that, and then faced forward. He looked up, gauged the sun, and thought it would be about an age before they finally had sight of Ashacre.

As he lowered his eyes back toward the road, he couldn't help but deride the landscape. As far as the eye could see, there were sloping, rolling low hills full of long, wild grain farmed by no one, and punctuated with the occasional group of aspen trees. Given the overall haze of today's not-quite-midmorning sky, every vista before him seemed like the last. It did nothing to help him stave off the long thoughts that stalked toward his waking mind.

-III-

Swordsmen stood beside me,
Lords of fen and field,
Smiled to risk their bones,
Each man a living shield.

Kaith felt the impact of something massive colliding against his shield. He'd braced his shoulder, and for a wonder, his position held. Blows from weapons rarely made the bones and muscles of his shield arm vibrate so completely.

In more standard engagements, the largest danger came from clever strikes that forced the shield off its normal center of balance, maneuvering the bulwark to one side or another in an effort to create an opening in an otherwise solid defense. The sheer force of the impact made it clear that a body of some considerable weight had been thrown against him.

To his right, Lamwreigh's shield came uncoupled from Kaith's for just a moment. It wasn't fear that had unbalanced Lamwreigh, merely the youth's comparative weight when held up against the enemy that had rammed their shield wall.

"No, you don't!" Robis said. His words were quickly delivered, though spoken with a surprising and bitter calm that knew nothing of age. He pulled back his glaive and set it diagonally against Lamwreigh's back to brace him, preventing him from sliding any further. "I have you. Now dress that damned line!"

Lamwreigh didn't have to be told twice. With a grunt, he shoved forward locking his shield into position between Kaith's and Samik's.

To his left, Kaith felt Valgar shift, rolling so his back was against Kaith's left shoulder.

"Robis!" Valgar shouted, "Refuse the left! Get somebody over here to help me! There's a damned *horse* breaking through!"

"Aye, I see it," came Greggor's voice. He was *almost* as calm as ever, but his words were slightly more clipped than usual as he raced along behind their line.

Kaith heard a grunt of effort, the clatter of hooves, and a sickly wet popping noise.

"Valgar? Your sword, if you please?" Greggor was both strained and insistent, despite the requisite understatement of his dry wit. He sounded as if he was struggling under a mighty weight.

"Kaith! Refuse the left. Close it up!"

"Refuse the left, aye!" Kaith's response was swift and automatic. "Lamwreigh, stay the line."

As Valgar took a step behind the shield wall, Kaith was already bending back, making the line's flank look like the left side of a trapezoid. As he finished the act of repositioning himself, he saw what Greggor had done. Sir Reginald's white warhorse (its chest mauled, dripping gore and ribbons of flesh) had managed to lumber into their backfield. The men had decided earlier that day that the poor thing's bulk was too heavy to effectively move into the moat with the other corpses. Now it looked like all of them were paying for that decision. Greggor's glaive had penetrated the thing's neck, and could now be seen poking out from the top of its head. Unfortunately, the wound didn't appear to be doing more than inconveniencing the grotesque mount.

Valgar took a single step to Kaith's left, Greggor's right. In relative silence, Valgar brought his sword down just below where the glaive exited the top of the horse's head. It took him several strokes before the animal's head finally parted ways with its neck, but at long last, the creature collapsed.

"The heads!" Kaith shouted, "Take their heads and they'll fall to the ground like any other thing in creation! Take their heads!"

"Glaives! Spears! Shift right!" Greggor barked.

As always, the men echoed the call, then executed the command.

The thing pressing against Kaith and Lamwreigh's shields seemed to slip off to the left suddenly.

"Valgar!?" If Kaith was right, the thing that *had been* pressing against both shields with such vehemence was going to shift to its right, rushing straight toward Valgar's turned back.

He needn't have worried. Valgar spun, charged forward with his shield before him, and punched his shield upward, catching the beast's lower jaw and knocking it off balance.

Wasting no time, he shoved the creature directly into the burning guardhouse to the left.

Kaith had been right, it had been a wolf—perhaps even a massive Winter Wolf—though not of the same coloring as he'd seen on Forester's once-foe. *Had been* was certainly the operative phrase, now.

Seeing that gave him an idea. Kaith made his voice sharp to be heard clearly above the din.

"Valgar! Slot in!"

Valgar shouted his assent, backpedaled to stand on Kaith's left, locked his shield in position, and waited to replace Kaith in the line.

Kaith disengaged once Valgar was braced, shouting, "Dress the line!" as he moved.

As always, the men echoed the order and executed the command. Once he was satisfied that Valgar was in place (which took all of an eyeblink) Kaith stepped back behind the line of reach weapons that made up the second rank, holding his sword aloft. It would serve to focus those who looked to identify who was giving the order. If the enemy had archers, this would've been a foolish, if not suicidal decision, marking him as a prime target.

Speaking of archers, he heard more arrows being loosed overhead, toward either flank of the town—Yaru and Arafad doing their best to provide their war effort with missile support.

"Shield wall!" Kaith bawled, "Give me a wedge! Tip of the spear! Aethan, center! Samik! Left! Barnic! Right! Move-move-move!"

At once the command was echoed. In a matter of seconds, the men had formed themselves into a very small chevron shape. Kaith saw Barnic move to cover the flank, dispatching more shambling creatures as range allowed. Jastar and his nine-foot spear slotted into position just behind.

"Alnik?" Greggor's voice, loud but reassuringly in control.

The sound of his name stopped his uncertain shift toward the western flank before it'd really started. "Stand fast! Never move a step! You're *just* where I want you: right behind Aethan!"

The brown-eyed constable (until recently Westsong's only regularly armed man) nodded and reset both stance and spear. He looked as if he were managing well, despite being utterly out of his element. He alone was unused to fighting within a larger force. Greggor had, therefore, wisely put him in the center of the pole weapons, where his eye could focus on targets in spear range, rather than trying to mentally contend with the entire field.

Normally, tunnel vision in combat was most deadly to the one seeing through it. In this case, however, Alnik had a force between him and the enemy. He couldn't afford to be oblivious, but his lack of experience in small unit tactics and formations would do everyone far less harm with him near the center of the rear rank.

"Kaith?" Raun's voice was full of uncertainty. He didn't see it yet. Fortunately, Kaith had been drawing breath to give the next order, even as the bard was calling his name.

"We're going to shove them into the fires! Keep reforming, keep dressing the line! Poles, make ready to brace the shields!" He drew a deep breath, took a step back to take in the field one final time, and gave the order.

"Shield wall! Advance by step! Step-step-step-step-step, line stop!" The men echoed his order, shouting the word *step* right along with him until the command to stop had been issued. He saw a dozen men and beasts undertake what could only be described as a shambling charge across the bridge.

He'd stopped his formation just in time.

"Brace!" He'd planned to say the word two or three times, as was the norm, but there hadn't been time. They'd braced their wall of tower shields just before the dead things impacted. "Stay the line!" He fought to maintain the surety in his voice, despite the enemy grabbing at, and trying to dislodge the tight formation's cohesion.

"Stay the line!" he said again. There were only two more left to join the shambling, groping mob, and one of them was the ruined form of Sir Reginald. He hoped Robis's vantage meant he would be spared the sight of his sire stagger-striding toward them, but hope was all he had time for. "Now! Into the fires! Now! Now! Thorion!"

Screaming as one, screaming "Thorion!" they obeyed.

-IV-

"Who are you thinking about?" Raun's voice, soft though it was, forced him back from the memory of that bloody cadence.

"Raun." Kaith nodded as the man rode up beside him.

"Kaith..." His voice held a hint of quiet annoyance for the formality, minor though it was. He let a minute pass in silence, their horses ambling along amiably enough. At length, he asked his question again.

"Who are you thinking about?"

"Does it matter?" Kaith's voice was more defensive than he would've liked, but the words were already out of his mouth. He didn't mind. He wanted silence with his thoughts, not prodding questioning...

"I keep thinking about Samik," Raun said. "It's hard to believe a mountain like that..."

Kaith's voice was sharp as it cut across him. "Must we?"

Raun rode in silence, his face expressionless.

"I'm sorry," Kaith said eventually.

"It's fine," Raun said. He sounded like he meant it, which made Kaith feel even worse. "I'm just trying to find the right way to honor them."

"When the Falx comes..." said Kaith, beginning the old catechism.

"Burn the Falx!" Raun said. His voice was black and bitter, almost angry.

"Burn the—"

Raun cut him off before he could finish, his voice the auditory equivalent of wrapping one's bare hand round a thorn bush. "Falx, yes Kaith. Burn the damned thing. Burn it, hang it, throw it off a cliff!" He returned to riding in silence for perhaps a minute before resuming in a less agitated tone. "I'm not trying to make sense of their deaths, or their lives, Kaith. I'm not looking for a bedtime story that lets me lay them down in peace at last."

"What, then?"

"I don't know," Raun said, voice returning to its normal, softer tone. "Something to keep them alive?"

Kaith looked at him, uncertainty etched across his face.

"That's not *remotely* what I meant." Raun snorted in spite of himself. "I mean a statue, an entry in the great histories and sagas, I don't know..."

"...a song?"

Raun blinked hard, then hung his head, nodding.

"Already tried, have you?" Kaith's voice was low and sympathetic—was almost another apology.

"It's too big for me." Raun nodded. "I can set the stage, but everything that comes out after that, it's just hollow. It doesn't do the battle justice, nor the loss, nor the valor they displayed."

"Well," said he, "Maybe that's enough."

Raun eyed him. "Enough?"

"Yes, Raun. Setting the scene. Taking everyone to the moment before the first charge. Maybe that's enough." He paused for a moment, looking down and studying his horse's mane as he collected his thoughts. "Before long, the whole county will know what happened at Westsong. There'll be records of the Countess's proclamations before the battle for both the living and the dead. There'll be a library's worth of information written down, and what's written down is discussed and debated for years, decades, perhaps longer."

"A song that takes everybody to the moment before they charged our line, however..." Raun trailed off, then nodded. "Maybe you're right. Thank you, brother."

Kaith nodded agreeably enough. After a moment he asked one final question.

"What will you call it?"

"Silver in the Skies, I think."

Kaith cocked his head to the side, rolling the words around in his mind. Raun was eying him, trying to gauge his reaction. At length, he put the singer out of his misery.

"Silver in the Skies. I like it." Kaith wrapped his fist around the silver chain he wore, meeting Raun's eyes. "I like it very well."

-V-

Spear and glaive behind me,
Deadly, swift and strong,
Wraiths of winter's moon above,
Fade ragged, and are gone.

"Horses!" Robis shouted. He shoved Samik out of the way just before the charge would've run him down. How he'd managed to move the mountain of a man was a matter quite beyond comprehension, but he had. Samik now owed Robis his life. It was a debt he'd never be able to repay.

"Scatter!" Barnic's shout was a sudden thunderclap.

Kaith's impromptu wedge had worked to shove the shambling, shuffling things into the fires set within the moat. First to be devoured by the flames was Sir Reginald. Kaith had seen him starting to raise both his sword and his chin, as if to give an order, when the wave of bodies hit him, driven by the press of their shields. It had been effective, certainly, but he hadn't correctly reckoned when and if Sir Cedric's cavalry would at last cross the bridge and enter the fray. It seemed like the fire had been keeping them at bay, and they'd been content to send other troops in to tire Westsong's few defenders. Either they had run out of additional troops to send or the mounted creatures had run out of patience. Once the eight horses—*hadn't there been only six when we lit the fires?* Kaith thought—had managed to plow through, and were in the courtyard, Marcza's voice rang out clear.

"Form up! Form up! Back them against the manor! Hem them in! Now! Move-move-move!"

Kaith spun to face toward the manor and the invading horsemen. He saw Lamwreigh's brother Lanian stand on the back of his father's horse, then leap onto the wall of the manor, beginning to climb the ivy.

"Cedric is alone! I'll keep him that way!" Kaith was surprised at his own bravado, but knew he had the right of it. An effective leader on the field was a force multiplier for even a handful of soldiers. Cedric would have to be kept isolated if he couldn't be outright removed. "Give me a triad, Marcza!"

Lamwreigh thumped into position along Kaith's right, locking his shield into place.

"On your right, Kaith! I'm with you!"

Kaith nodded. "Be ready to move, double-time! Now to grab a glaive or spear."

As if his words had summoned the man...

"Spear in, Kaith! Jastar's with you!"

Kaith's smile was bitter as he tightened his grip on both sword and shield. This, he could do. This was just another tournament. Small units versus large, infantry versus cavalry. He readied himself, drawing a draft of rain-thickened air before letting it out in a burst of sound.

"Cedric!" As one, Kaith and Lamwreigh sped toward the darksome knight. As one, they dipped down as they began the last few steps that would take them into combat range. Two strides later, they pistoned forward and upward, driving their shields with the full weight of their rising bodies. They collided with the left side of Sir Cedric's horse, pinning his leg to it, somehow unbalancing the creature.

As the horse stumbled to the right, they pressed the advantage their momentum had granted them. They posted their tower shields high, trying to limit their foe's angles of attack while giving Jastar a clear target.

They'd denied Sir Cedric's favorite angle of attack by the positioning of the two massive shields. The hammer shot, as it was known, was a simple, swift, downward strike. When executed correctly, it served to drive shields or skulls Skolfward like tent stakes in soft earth. In this case, however, the shields had been posted too high.

Sir Cedric, instead, began throwing scorpion's-tail-like shots with his broadsword, trying to angle the edge of his blade so that it cut into the backs of the shieldmen or the head of the spearman.

Kaith automatically angled his sword into a dump block, using it and his gauntlet to cover the back of his head and spine. He hoped Lamwreigh was doing the same.

"My son is a traitor!" Cedric said. His voice was as plain and detached as it had been before dawn when the true siege had begun.

Jastar stepped back, using every one of the nine feet that made up the length of his spear. He stabbed Cedric over, and over again, but the dead thing kept right on speaking: hurling sword strikes, taunts and the detached, but somehow still disgusted disappointment of a nightmare wearing a father's face.

Finally, Sir Cedric grabbed the haft of Jastar's spear with his gauntleted left hand, yanking it out of his grasp with an inhuman strength.

"No!" Lamwreigh stepped back, separating his shield from Kaith's. He punched it upward anew; knocking the spear aside before it could be spun and aimed at its original owner. He then leapt upward and forward, slamming his shield into Sir Cedric's side, and smacking him into the wall of the manor, unceremoniously throwing him from his ghoulish mount.

"Jastar! Take its reins! Lead it into the fire!"

"Aye, Kaith!" A moment later, the dead horse was led away without a sound of protest. Later, Kaith would find that image chilling—how the thing had gone along, docile as you please, even into the fire.

With the horse's bulk no longer in the way, Kaith's eyes fell upon the final grim contest between father and son. There before the manor's eastern bay window, Lamwreigh had pinned Sir Cedric's body to the ground with his tower shield.

He'd dimly registered the fact that he could no longer see anyone in the lower windows—not that he blamed them for fleeing deeper into the manor at this point—before he called his name, running to the youth's side.

His heart sank as Lamwreigh screamed in desperation, begging Kaith to act, to do what he could not.

"Kaith! Kaith, you have to do it!" Even as Lamwreigh called out, the unearthly strength of the thing that wore his father's face was nearly able to overpower him. Sir Cedric was lifting his son bodily, shield and all, even as Lamwreigh pressed down with all of his weight.

Kaith didn't ask what Lamwreigh meant. It was unnecessary. Lamwreigh could help, could hold his father's animated body down, could even fight him, but he couldn't be the one to take his head.

Kaith tried to steel himself for the grim task as he crossed the remaining few feet that separated them. He'd killed men before (bandits and raiders mostly), but a Knight of Thorion, a once-good man, well respected throughout the County?

Holding his breath, forcing himself to look into Sir Cedric's mad, monstrous eyes, Kaith raised his sword and struck.

As his head came away from his neck, Sir Cedric adopted an expression of peace and tranquility that Kaith thought he'd never forget. It was as if, in the final moment of his second life, Cedric of Eastshadow was relieved to be allowed to truly find rest.

Lamwreigh got to his feet, his eyes swimming with unshed tears.

"Thank you," he managed. If the youth had more to say, this wasn't the time.

A man (what had only recently been a man) rode up from the east and dismounted, calling Lamwreigh's name. An instant later, he was joined by a second, then a third, this time riding in from the south.

"Back to back!" Kaith tried to keep the fear out of his voice. Lamwreigh complied, but far more slowly than was prudent.

The first of Sir Cedric's former men-at-arms to arrive batted Lamwreigh shield aside, opening his defense with an almost lazy back cut (a horizontal sweep from dim to bright-hand side). He lunged forward to take full advantage of the defenseless youth, but was shouldered out of the way by a black blur of motion holding a glaive.

"Robis!" Lamwreigh's voice was a study in shocked surprise.

Kaith circled with the undead (*Squire? Had this thing been a squire not long up the hourglass? No, no silver chain— just a groom or other such armsman*) that engaged him, trying to maneuver him so that he could watch the rest of the battlefield.

At sixteen, Robis's reflexes were near their peak. His momentum carried him forward, his glaive nearly a blur as he spun and stabbed it this way and that. He moved like a whirlwind, dancing, distracting, almost toying with his foes. He separated one attacker from the other, then herded the two of them together toward the wall of the manor house, then separated them once again, his body never still for more than a moment.

An inhuman scream came from the second floor of the manor, causing each of them to risk a glance upward.

Something came hurtling out of the second-story window. Arafad (framed in that great portal just a moment ago) was nowhere to be found. The object rag-dolled, arced upward and outward from the manor, tumbling end over end as it fell.

No, not an object, a body, Kaith realized. *A girl of perhaps six or seven. Likely one-half of that Window's watchers.*

Lamwreigh looked up. He tossed his massive shield to the side and leapt to try to catch the girl as she fell.

The creature that'd nearly killed Sir Cedric's eldest son (before being engaged by the storm wind named Robis) took advantage of the falling distraction. The dead swordsman disengaged from the youth's spinning glaive, leaving his grim companion to fend Robis off. He lunged at Lamwreigh. His sword arm executed a flat snap (a horizontal strike from bright to dim-hand side) on target to remove Lamwreigh's head.

Kaith tried to step past his own foe, but whoever he'd been in life, he was inhumanly fast on his feet. Kaith saw the blow coming and understood that Lamwreigh would die. There was nothing Kaith could do to save him.

So ends the line of Eastshadow, he thought. *Lamwreigh, I've failed you. How do I live with that?*

Robis leapt into motion, somehow interposing his glaive between the strike and Lamwreigh's head. Unfortunately, doing so cost him.

The foe he'd disengaged with now lunged forward to take advantage of Robis's distraction. He drove his sword up through the youth's kidney its point erupting from Robis's chest like the prow of a ship finally emerging from an eerie midnight fog.

Lamwreigh opened his mouth to scream, but nothing came out. The girl forgotten, he leapt past Robis's dying form and engaged his killer, hammering him back with blow after blow.

Channeling all of his mingled rage and grief, Kaith rammed his shield into the man-at-arms he was fighting, driving him back toward the skolfbound girl and knocking him off balance. As he'd hoped, his foe fell sprawling directly (or nearly directly) in line to cushion her landing. The impact would hurt, would likely break bone, and knock her unconscious, but it would be softer than landing on the bare flagstones.

She landed in a heap, making a sickening, wet sound.

Kaith took a giant step forward, spinning his sword so that its blade was inverted. Screaming an inarticulate battle cry, he managed to drive it down into his foes head, forcing a comical look of abject surprise to bloom on the dead thing's face before it, too, bore that look of peace he'd seen on Sir Cedric's still features.

Breathing hard, releasing the hilt of his sword (leaving it, for the moment, to stick out of his blessedly still foe's mouth), Kaith knelt to check on the girl.

He gently pulled her into a sitting position, his arm around her shoulders to steady her. Her head lolled forward, chin on chest, and there was a dark stain running down the center of her gray sackcloth dress.

He struggled to find his voice. Before he could speak, however, she lifted her head. Her eyes were glassy and unblinking: two shocked and beautiful emeralds. She opened her mouth to smile at him, missing a few front teeth, and then it happened. All the color drained from her face, chased by a pale, moon-kissed blue. Her arms lifted, the colors racing each other toward her fingertips. Between eye blinks; her nails elongated, becoming first yellowed, then darkening to the color of dried blood. She tried to sink them into his neck, lunging forward with surprising speed, and a mouth full of irregular fangs.

His gorget saved him from that initial assault. An odd, sweet smell of rot wafted up from where she had gouged his leather collar. He stood up, never meaning to do so, and moved his arm so that he could grab the girl by the back of her dress near its neckline. He held her at bay as if she were an angry kitten, lifted by the scruff of her neck.

That act of nearly comedic self-defense was a distant and automatic thing. His mind was reeling, teetering over an internal precipice. What was he doing here? He'd been right—he was no knight.

She continued to snarl and spit, bite and claw at him, but he held her out of reach of anything vital. Looking past her, he saw Lamwreigh had dispatched the thing that had killed Robis and was now engaged with the last of the grim folk that had once been his friends and training partners.

A chill passed over Kaith as his eyes left the ruined, blue mockery of the once-girl. He cast about himself, assessing the battlefield. Rain pelted down, the sky full of clouds so heavy that they seemed to be reaching from on-high with a slobbering, sickening intent. The sky's malice fell on Robis's limp form.

Kaith had seen the first of them to fall, and it had been a boy he himself had helped to train. He remembered Robis rushing toward him in the stable complex, full of pride and good humor after his tournament victory—remembered him in the sun, looking out at her Excellency's horses, his arm companionably around Lamwreigh's shoulders. How had he been the first? How had Kaith allowed him to fall?

With a shudder of muted horror, he realized that he didn't actually know if that were true or not.

He looked across the stony urban battlefield and saw his brothers and sister-in-arms capering amidst the knife-like downpour and unfettered firelight. As they fought their own skirmishes in the middle distance, surrounded by foes too numerous to count (*where in hells have they all come from? There were only eight horsemen, and four of them are here with Lamwreigh and I*), he wrestled with a dawning truth. Robis could have been the first or the fourteenth casualty on this hellish field. He wouldn't, couldn't know while the fighting lasted. Some were still left. Some still held their desperate courage to the rain-soaked sticking place ... but how many? Was Robis the first to fall? The fourth? Was he simply one of many already dead in a final act of service to the Thorion throne?

He heard Jastar in combat to the south with another of their former countrymen and fought back the wave of despair that threatened to overtake him. Suddenly the immortality they'd all felt at the beginning of the battle seemed to have washed away in the flood. He wanted to weep, to throw down his arms and give in to the inevitable.

He looked at the once-girl again, snarling and growling in her impotence at the end of his outstretched arm. Hearing Lamwreigh bleat Robis's name in grief and horror, Kaith couldn't help but wonder what hope they truly had. Coming out of this alive, let alone victorious, seemed a bitter joke—all but a laughable impossibility.

CHAPTER FIVE

THE RED FOG OF EASTSHADOW

-I-

Kaith and Raun rode in silence for the better part of an hour. Kaith's mind wandered and seemed helpless to do anything but relive the battle. Distantly, he heard the boy shouting, "Catch me!" over and over again. For a moment it seemed like it was coming from all around him.

Eventually he turned his head to look at Raun, beside him in the saddle, and when the other man's mouth moved, he heard Lanian's voice again, coming out of it.

"Catch me!" His voice was a high, clear cry, manic and full of a joy that twisted into something hungry and sadistic.

"What!?"

Raun looked startled at Kaith's sharp tone and wild-eyed half-glare. His expression, however, was born of concern for his old friend (or new brother, if that better served) not terror. He hadn't heard the voice.

"I said I'm going to try and catch sleep. I rode beside the Countess's carriage for an hour or two before coming up here. I'm really starting to feel it, and thought I'd go find a replacement—are you alright, Kaith?" Raun's concern was so sudden, so fervently genuine that his question rushed out from between his teeth before he'd finished his previous sentence.

"As much as anyone else here, yes. Go get some sleep." Kaith tried to smile. It felt alien on his face. It felt as if he'd fallen asleep in the middle of an open field with the sun blazing down. His skin was too tight, somehow. He suspected it was fire-reddened, as when, as a small boy, he'd stood too close to his father's forge. A good many of them seemed to have that cast to their skin. A gift from fighting so close to the pyres they'd made of Westsong.

After confirming that Kaith was certain, Raun took his leave. While Kaith waited for the man's replacement, he once again found himself thinking back, hearing Lanian's voice, far and wee in the back of his mind.

"Catch me!"

-II-

Lit by Westsong's last autumn fires, the blood-kissed sky stole the moon, diffusing its ragged silver glow amidst the low-slung storm clouds as they spat endless, freezing rain upon the town's last defenders.

"Catch me!" Lanian shouted, voice gleeful.

Kaith's head snapped upward—he was helpless not to. He saw the boy leap from the second-story window, the one from which the girl had been thrown. Lanian's face wore an incongruously sunny grin, as if he were jumping from the loft of a barn into a pile of newly mown hay. As he fell, the top of the manor house exploded in bright, white fire.

Kaith didn't think, he reacted. He drew the arm holding the girl back across his own body, twisting at the waist. She tried to grab his arm, then his shoulder, but there simply wasn't time for her to get a strong grip. Shrieking inarticulately, he flung the girl directly at the falling form of Lanian in hopes to divert his suicidal jump.

Kaith's aim had been true enough, but Lanian wasn't struck by the girl. Instead, he caught her in midair, landing deftly on his feet a few yards away from where Lamwreigh was fighting.

For a moment, it looked as if the boy were going to thrust the dead girl away from him, for he had stretched out his arms, distancing her from the center mass of his body. A heartbeat later, however, he twirled her around as small children had been twirled for years uncounted by parents and older siblings. For three revolutions he spun her, slowing as he ended, bringing her to rest against his chest, arms under her bottom, laughing delightedly.

In that moment, Lanian *almost* sounded the way he looked—like a boy of ten. The girl, too, stopped her feral snarling and giggled as she rode in his arms, her hands now clasped behind his neck. Her laughter made it sound as if, at some signal, she'd stopped playing whatever game had previously taken her fancy, and now that it was over, was being taken away by the infectious amusement that seemed to be the sole purview of children.

As for Lanian, there was something unhinged and insane about his laughter. As it had been when the siege had begun before dawn, it was jagged and unnerving. It scratched at the secret places of the mind, scrabbling for purchase.

"What an excellent throw!" Lanian chided. He'd barely managed to get the taunt out amidst the peals of laughter that continued to erupt from his slight frame.

As Kaith's hand found the hilt of his sword again, muscles working to remove it from the twice-dead thing he'd last used it on, his mind finally accepted what his ears had been hearing. The boy's voice wasn't the only one coming out of his mouth. There was a lower, deeper, more guttural voice underpinning his every word and every sound.

Lamwreigh dispatched the last of Sir Cedric's immediate retinue. Turning to look for a new foe, his eyes fell on the children. Lowering his sword, he walked toward them.

"You have to put a stop to this," he said.

"No – I – don't!" The boy delivered this well-reasoned response in a kind of singsong. The dead girl in his arms giggled at Lanian's snotty, mocking tone.

"Lanian, look what you've made me do!" Lamwreigh's voice was angry and incredulous. "I've had to kill all of Father's men and see to Father's own end!"

Absurdly, Lamwreigh sounded very much as if he were disciplining his younger brother, explaining to him firmly what he'd done wrong and why he was to be punished. Absurd or not, his voice was both firm and steady. All trace of the childish tears which had been swimming in his eyes for most of tonight's fighting was gone. It wasn't as if he'd cast his woe aside. It was as if he'd never worn it in the first place.

"So?" Lanian laughed. "He was too old and tired anyway. As for Hamian," he looked past him to the body of Lamwreigh's most recent sparring partner, "...who you finally bested I see, and the rest of father's old guard, they were all useless!"

Lamwreigh was horrified. He crossed most of the remaining distance between them, inverted his sword, and drove it to the ground point first. Dropping to one knee, he positioned himself so they were at eye level with one another, a mere yard between them.

"That's simply not true!"

"It's absolutely true," Lanian said. His voice had lost most of its jocularity, and as he put the once-girl in his arms down beside him, still holding her hand, he regarded his brother with a gaze that spoke of a strained species of pity. "Half of them would have put a knife in your back or poison in your wine if they thought it would serve their purposes. Who will miss them? We're finally free! Don't you understand that? We were only waiting for Father to die so you could take over as Lord of Eastshadow."

"Lanian, you're wrong." Lamwreigh's voice strove for calm and to maintain the authority his additional five years of life should have granted him.

"I'm not. It was always meant to be that you sat in judgment over the people of Eastshadow, and I stood at your right hand, whispering in your ear. I've always been smarter than you, and you've always been a better warrior." Lanian paused for a moment to look in Kaith's direction. The body of Sir Cedric was only a few feet beyond. "Father was a fool. He was more concerned about petty, surface politics than real power. He learned only enough about battle and intimidation to impress those directly around him."

"Father was content because he had already achieved greatness. He was well respected at court, well respected on the tournament field, well respected in times of war or strife against goblins or bandits. He was even successful at arranging betrothals for both you and I, expanding the power and influence of our household and securing our future... Lanian, where is this nonsense coming from? Who's told you to speak so?"

Kaith could see a single but steady stream of arrows raining down from the upper floors into the crowd of dead things his brothers and sister were fighting to the east of the manor. Either Arafad or Yaru had survived the explosion of the top floor, it seemed.

He heard Marcza's clear voice barking commands, though he couldn't make any of them out.

There were still so damned many of them!

As if in answer, Kaith saw one of the once-men across the yard, backlit by the inferno of the moat, raise his left hand, palm out. He was suddenly flanked by two more shapes—men who hadn't been there a moment before, he would have sworn.

Replacing that fresh horror with one closer at hand, he saw movement a few feet to his left, close to the manor house wall.

Slowly, Robis began to stand up. He cast about for a moment before his eyes fell upon Kaith. He tried a weak, tired species of that quicksand smile, nearly managing it before his face registered panic.

"Kaith?" Robis's tone was one of wheezing confusion. "Kaith, help ... me—" No sooner had this desperate request escaped Robis's lips than Kaith again witnessed the dreadful change, just as he had in the girl. Robis's young and handsome face grew pale and then was suffused with that moon-kissed, blue misery, twisting into a feral snarl.

Lanian's tone grew bitter and disappointed. Kaith could hear it even as he turned to square off with Robis.

"Oh Lamwreigh," he began. "You're just like him. He made too much of his wine, practiced at powerlessness."

"I am the heir," Lamwreigh snapped. "I am the elder brother, the eldest son, and I will not suffer you to speak ill of our father."

"I'm not speaking ill of him, Lamwreigh, I'm speaking the truth of him."

From the corner of his eye, Kaith registered the boy shake his head and brush back the hair from his brow before continuing in a maddeningly reasonable tone.

"Our father confused a child's authority over his play-mates with the real thing. He believed the respect of a few manorial knights when he should happen to come into contact with them was equal to ruling over them and commanding their loyalty." Though his voice still ran before him in a child's high tones, his words, his diction, even his obvious grasp of these insanely adult arguments, was striking. He might have been thirteen or thirty, reading from some great political philosopher's text, rather than a boy of ten. Of course, the boy of ten had shown agility, endurance, and a control over undeniably dark magics that made questions of his age irrelevant.

Kaith was doing his best to fend off Robis's attacks using just his shield. He knew it was foolish. The true Robis had already passed beyond any fear of pain Kaith might bring him. Still, he found himself trying not to hurt the youth.

Through eyes that swam with misery and grief, he saw Samik over Robis's shoulder, across the courtyard. A towering mass of muscle, Kaith could make him out easily as he picked up men and beasts alike, carried them several feet, and threw them bodily into the fires of the moat. As he turned around to go back to the fray from one such sojourn, he saw Kaith and raised a hand. Picking up his shield from the ground where it lay nearby, he sprinted across the thirty feet of intervening courtyard and opened his mouth to shout.

"K-k-k-kuh," Samik began. He growled, hitting himself in the head with his free hand, and tried again. "K-K-Kuh-Kuh-Kaith!" His face split in a wild, relieved smile before he pressed on. "Command!" He both nodded his head and thumbed back over his shoulder to where the bulk of their forces were still engaged with the ambling, snarling dead. Unless his eyes were deceiving him, the number of foes his fellows were contending with had grown again and by no small amount.

As Kaith opened his mouth to protest, his eyes flitting toward Robis, Samik reverted to gesture. He shook his head at Kaith, pointed to Robis, and hefted his own shield as he picked around the corpses which were, blessedly, no longer moving.

Lanian watched this with mild interest, reached down to take the little dead girl's other hand, and, taking a leaf from Kaith's own book, he hurled her with inhuman strength directly onto Samik.

"No!" Lamwreigh's shock and horror bloomed even as the little girl soared over his head.

Lamwreigh had done well to warn Samik, but had shouted the wrong word.

"Samik! Left!" Kaith bawled. The command was correct, but even as he'd issued it, he knew it'd come far too late.

Samik spun, surprised, and tried to bring his shield up to cover his left side—but seeing a child flying at him, he hesitated, half-opening his arms to catch her.

She fell into his waiting, half-hearted embrace, uneven fangs first bared, then sinking into his throat by way of the shelf under his massive chin. He fell an instant later, gurgling.

Kaith wanted to move, wanted to run over, wanted to help him, to do *something*. He knew, however, that if he let go of Robis, he would be forced...Would be forced...

To do what, exactly? Robis was already dead. Kaith was no sorcerer. He'd held some vainglorious hope that he might be able to find a way to... what, restore Robis to life? Had he truly thought he could somehow relight the spark that had driven Robis to fight with such speed, ferocity, and heart? Surely he wasn't that arrogant, was he?

Kaith found that he was, or at least that he had been. His heart sank. What was he doing? He was again reminded of his first thought upon the Countess calling him into service. He was a smith's son. He had a talent for melee combat and was accounted clever by even Greggor, which was high praise indeed, but a knight?

-III-

Kaith heard Lamwreigh's voice. It pulled him out of the depressed futility that threatened to swallow him once again. His head snapped toward the sound, even as his body continued to strive to keep Robis at bay.

"Lanian," Lamwreigh half cried, and half growled his brother's name. "I am the elder brother. I am the heir to the house of Eastshadow! You will obey me! You will stop this madness, and you will do it now!"

Lanian had opened his mouth in another of those far-too-wide grins. The expression fell away as if Lamwreigh's voice had been a slap. His face suddenly became serious. As he spoke, he bowed his head in contrition, his voice small and wee.

"Get up, Lamwreigh," said he. "I can't bear to see you on your knees."

"Then *stop this...* Put an *end* to all of this, *now*."

Lamwreigh's voice was soft, insistent, and pleading.

Kaith could see on his face that he'd heard the shuffling behind him. He'd registered the sound and knew that Samik was rising. He locked eyes with his brother, held his gaze for twin heartbeats, and spoke a final word: "...Please."

Lanian met his brother's eyes for a moment, bowed his head, then nodded. "Am I your brother, still?"

"Always," said he.

"I'm yours and you're mine?" Lanian's voice grew softer still, choked and brittle. He sounded as if he were struggling to stave off sobs.

Lamwreigh nodded, his face wet with fear and hope in equal measure.

"You're still my brother, even after all of this. Father's gone. It's my job to look after you now. Whatever dark *thing* is inside of you, banish it, let it out, send it away. It doesn't own you. It's as you say. I'm yours and you're mine."

The roof of the manor house collapsed. The fire had burned away enough that the entire second story could no longer support its own weight. As the upper floor fell in, Kaith was pelted by falling and flaming debris. He briefly lost his footing. As he stumbled backward, desperately trying to maintain his balance, Robis shoved forward, causing Kaith to fall on his back with enough force to snap his teeth together with an audible click.

He brought his shield up to bear, covering the majority of his prone form, and then smelled burning flesh.

Lanian spoke as if nothing had happened. He still sounded close to unmoored, but it was as if the destruction that surrounded them held no power over him.

"Very well. Embrace me then. If I'm really still your brother, embrace me. Promise you'll keep me safe."

Kaith rolled up into a kneeling position, his shield in front of him then stood. He saw Robis, face down in front of him and burning. He'd stopped moving. Samik was burning as well, though he still stood a few feet away from the sons of Eastshadow. The once-girl's piteous form lay smoldering at his feet, mewling a final, feral whimper before it too fled flesh.

Kaith looked at the brothers, then caught Lamwreigh's eye as the youth laid his sword down at his side.

Voice hesitant, Kaith asked, "Lamwreigh? Is it over?"

Lamwreigh nodded. Standing, he strode the three or four feet that separated him from Lanian. He bent and scooped the boy into his arms, held him tightly, and cupped the back of his head with his right hand.

Lanian returned the embrace with a desperate abandon that suggested the boy was teetering on the edge of his mental and emotional limits. He laid his head on Lamwreigh's right shoulder, his arms and legs clinging tightly as if his life depended on it.

"I have you," Lamwreigh soothed. "I have you. I promise."

The Countess was suddenly there, standing framed in the manor's main entrance. She had a loaded crossbow in her hand, Kaith noted, though it was pointed down. Bruised and bloody, her face, hands, and hair showed obvious signs of being burned.

"Thank you, Lamwreigh," Lanian crooned. His cheeks were wet beneath his closed eyes, reflecting and softening the firelight. "I have to admit, I was wrong."

Lamwreigh eased the boys head back so he could look him in the face again. He was smiling the sort of relieved smile that only comes when a child is finally out of danger, safe at home.

"Did you really think I'd have abandoned you?" Lamwreigh asked this with a voice that was gentleness itself with no hint of accusation.

Lanian shook his head, smiling. He leaned forward so their foreheads touched. Through a contented sigh, he demurred.

"Of course not. It just turns out that I prefer you on your knees, after all."

As he said this, a muscular, guttural growl heralded an eruption of red vapor, as if it were being ripped from his mouth. It had small tines of violet lightning, little patches of bruising along its roiling red surface.

The boy's limbs still held him fast in his brother's arms, and Lamwreigh couldn't getaway. It forced its way into his mouth and nose, driving him down to his knees as Kaith watched helplessly.

When all the vapor had left the tiny body, Lanian's arms and legs released, and he fell backward onto the pavement as if he'd been thrown. He instantly began to cry and wail. "Give him back! Give him back!"

Then Kaith saw the terrible creeping change race across Lanian's face. His color was draining away, being replaced by that miserable, pallid blue. His voice, too, seemed to be draining away from cries of anguish and abandonment to high-pitched, growling, near-keening noises. They melded with the other screams Kaith began to hear, probably from behind the manor house, or worse, inside of it.

Time seemed to slow.

To the east side of the courtyard, he saw that there were now peasants trying to attack the armored men. He wondered, and not for the first time, how many of his brothers had fallen tonight. He wondered if his new sister, Marcza, had fallen. He wondered how long it would be until he fell. Even as the red cloud shoved the final inches of its bulk down Lamwreigh's throat, he doubted it would be long.

I can stomach fear, horror, and loss. I can suffer through fire, and rain, sleepless nights, and endless days, he thought. *I can command a battle line. I can kill men and monsters. I can even kill the dead for a second time. I don't know how I'd even begin to go about attacking a creature made of fog.*

His arms had grown heavy; his sword nearly ready to slip from his fingers, the strap of his shield already beginning to slide down his relaxing arm. It would be so much easier to just give over. There wasn't anything more he could do, was there?

A dull thump jarred him out of the despair that had nearly devoured him. He jerked his head up, looking toward the sound, and was astonished by the sudden silence that seemed to attack him.

The rain had stopped, as had the wind. The clouds were gone, not retreating or dissipating, but gone. The only song he could hear was that of the crackling fire all around him. Casting about, he saw Samik crumple to the ground, and further to the right the attacking peasants were doing the same. They didn't so much fall, as they collapsed as if they'd all passed out at the same time.

His eyes next fell on Lamwreigh who stood quivering on the spot a few feet away from him. The eldest son of Eastshadow opened his mouth to speak, and his voice came out in a husky whisper barely audible over the snap of the fires.

"Lanian? Lanian, I can't see."

With that, his legs buckled.

Kaith at once saw the difference between Lamwreigh and the collapsing townsfolk. A quarrel was sticking out from the back of the youth's head. It had bored into his skull and sunk nearly to the fletching.

Kaith cast his eyes to the Countess, still framed in the entrance to the manor house. She was still leaning in the door frame, holding the crossbow, its quarrel spent. Her countenance was that of bitter nobility, of a woman who had done what she needed to and was not for an instant sorry she'd done it.

"Yes, Sir Kaith," Ylspeth said. "It is over."

CHAPTER SIX

PUPPETS, PYRES, AND PATTERNS

-I-

The carriage trundled along at a goodish pace. It managed to be opulent without being ostentatious, its interior kept cool due to modest linen drapes which hung over every point of entry the light and heat of the day might otherwise find. Its seats (really little more than narrow, overstuffed, high-backed couches) were comfortable enough to sit or doze upon during the long hours spent traveling from settlement to settlement. It was, by any measure, a fitting way for any noble personage to travel.

For Ylspeth, Countess of Thorion, however, it always felt like a rolling coffin, or perhaps Skolf's most comfortable prison.

She'd been banished to this pleasant purgatory by those who served her, and who, she knew, truly cared about her well-being. She needed sleep, they said, or rest—what comfort could be offered. She knew they'd meant well. They only said such things because it seemed like the appropriate thing for them to do. The appropriate suggestion for them to make to show their gratitude, love, and devotion. She no longer wore the face of a young, vital, vibrant woman, after all. A reasonably polite way of saying she was officially considered past her childbearing years.

If they only knew...

They'd banished her so that she could sleep, though in truth sleep had been an art lost to her for almost as long as she could remember. Comfort? She wouldn't be comfortable until they were back in the county seat. There was too much to be done, and no ability to do it here on the road with so many refugees.

Still, there'd been nothing for it. If she'd insisted on sitting a horse for the entire trek between Westsong and Ashacre, the act would only have served to agitate the column. After what they'd all been through, she felt they were already shaken enough. So, she resigned herself to shamming sleep for a few hours, eyes closed, breathing steadily as her mind tried to make sense of all that she had seen, heard, and done last night.

It was necessary, she knew, to replay all that she could recall (which was most of it, blessedly) in order to best determine her next steps.

She'd begun to formulate a plan, of course. Still, she'd been taught to take as much time as she could, whenever she could, to assess a situation before committing to a course of action. She fervently believed in those teachings, and it had served her well for years uncounted now.

When, at last, she'd decided she could take no more—*would* take no more, she'd called the carriage to a halt, exited its maddening would-be comfort, and mounted upon a horse.

She rode toward the head of the column where she saw the newly minted Sir Kaith riding alone. As she approached, she allowed the weight of her thoughts to show both in her eyes, and on her face. Memory was a powerful tool, and she'd had much to think about since the attack. She would need to recruit others, bring some into her deeper councils—harvest the strength she'd planted to fortify herself and her designs, and soon.

Though she hated it, she'd also need to send word south, before they were overrun, and wouldn't *that* please her once-paramour? After so many years apart, she rued having to welcome him back into her good graces.

Good graces? No. That wasn't what this was. She would have to ask for his aid, and he would traipse back into her life like the conquering hero of a fairy tale come to rescue the damned damsel in distress. *That* was the real, hellish truth of it!

As she replayed the night's events for what felt like the eightieth time, she came to a grim conclusion. Westsong had only been a skirmish. The war itself wouldn't be long in coming.

-II-

Yaru and Arafad would have to die. She knew that. It was one thing for people to think of them as distant-eyed foreigners, capable warriors, and stoic conversationalists. It was another thing entirely for them to be lauded as heroes. That simply wouldn't do. Now that she'd knighted them, such accolades would mean they would be heralded, toasted endlessly, questioned on their political views ... wind and rain, they'd likely be drowning in would-be suitors, be expected to marry into the gentry.

Hells. She choked back a mouthful of bile. *After Westsong, they might be sought after to marry into the nobility, itself!*

It was regrettable. No—that was underselling it. It was a damnable shame, that was what it was!

Ylspeth cast a neutral gaze toward them. Their arms looked like waterwheels moving in a steady current. She watched as each in turn, reached down to pluck a new arrow out of one of the innumerable quivers laid beside them, nocked it, drew back, loosed it, and repeated the process with an uncanny and nearly inhuman rapidity. What was more, they showed no sign whatsoever of fatigue. Neither of the aged watchmen seemed to have noticed this, but one of the two children they'd been paired with kept glancing over, eyes shining with breathless wonder. One child noticing such skill could be dismissed and overlooked—probably would be by any adult the child happened to speak to. If the girl, on the other hand, drew her aged partner's attention while Yaru and Arafad continued their relentless activity...

No, they would have to die. It was a miserable, piteous thing, but there was nothing for it. She'd need to find an appropriate way to make that happen. The act itself was accomplished easily enough. The key was finding a way to accomplish it without being forced to kill the quartet that stood watch near at hand in the process.

Ylspeth saw that Yaru was beginning to run low on ammunition. She strode over to where he knelt and reached down to pluck a single arrow from his dwindling supply. Turning, she exited the room, walking down the hall to where she was normally expected to sleep.

Moving to her small hearth, she reached down to pluck a well-seasoned fagot from the pile.

She cradled the firewood in her arms as if it were a newborn, laying the arrow she plucked from Yaru's quiver on top of it as if it were the imaginary infant's favorite toy. She drew a deep breath down past her navel, held it for a three count, and released it in a slow, measured sigh. Once the majority of the air had been expelled; she turned on her heels and strode back down the hall to where the condemned archers plied their trade.

Crossing the room, she knelt by Yaru. Without a word, she began placing more than a score of new arrows into his quiver. The log she'd pulled from her supply of firewood was nowhere to be found.

"How much more ammunition can you render, Mistress?" Yaru's voice was somehow inhuman, like a tumble of stones somewhere high in the mountains, ominous and distant.

"Enough, Yaru. I shall bring more once I finish filling this quiver."

Yaru merely nodded, continuing to shoot with that same unearthly and unwavering speed.

Finishing her task, Ylspeth stood, casting an eye toward Arafad's equally diminishing supply of arrows, and scooped up empty quivers from each archer's store.

She hurried from the room, fleeing back down the hall to repeat the process and keep their supply of arrows from dwindling down to dangerous levels.

She'd no sooner finished converting the first new quiver's-worth than she'd heard first Robis, then Barnic shouting about horses. This was followed almost instantly by Marcza's bright, authoritative voice ordering the lot of them to reform.

Dropping the arrows into the first empty quiver to hand, she stood and ran back to the others.

Steps away from the opened door, a keening, terrified scream assaulted her ears.

Entering the chamber, her first thought was that the watchers were all dead. But no, that wasn't accurate. The remaining watchers were all dead. One of them, one of the children, was missing. It was the girl who'd been all eyes watching the archers at their work.

Well, at least that's settled, Ylspeth thought. *Not the end I'd wished for... but wishing won't return the key.*

Arafad lay on the ground halfway toward the rear of the chamber. He was slowly trying to get to his feet. The two old men and the young boy who'd made up the remainder of the watchers had landed in twisted heaps around the room. Their eyes were open, and they looked as if they'd died from fright or shock rather than violence.

Yaru, incongruously, stayed at his window and continued firing arrows as if nothing had happened.

Stood over the bodies of one old man and the boy (Ylspeth believed he might've been as old as five, but surely no more) was the youngest son of Sir Cedric of East shadow.

Lanian was in the center of the room, halfway between the sprawling Arafad and the kneeling machine that was Yaru. He beamed up as Ylspeth entered the chamber, eyes shining with the light, face upturned to her as if awaiting praise.

"Countess," he said by way of greeting. "I thought I might find you here." His tone was that of a child playing at courtly manners. It was the sort of tone one expected a boy to offer to an aunt, older sister, or first love as they entered into the dining hall, full of exaggerated courtesy.

Before she could speak, Arafad moved to a sitting position, and then to his feet.

The look on Lanian of Eastshadow's face was one of comic surprise. "What ...are you?" Lanian asked this question more to himself than to the newly upright Arafad.

Ylspeth saw his eyes glaze over, then glow a somehow noisome blue. As Arafad looked down at him with an air of curiosity, but a fatal lack of concern, Lanian mouthed an "Ahhh" before turning his full attention back to Ylspeth.

"Hello ... acolyte,"

Ylspeth held her eyes closed for just a moment. When she opened them again, things became much clearer. She saw the small, rock-like anthropomorphs superimposed over the chests of both Yaru and Arafad, just as she'd expected. The general alienness of their true form stood in stark contrast to the room, but it held no wonder for her. Why should it? They were as she had made them a scant three moons up the hourglass—Skolfish stone given false faces and the semblance of souls. The boy, too, had something superimposed over his slender form. She could see a tall, willowy, blood-colored creature wearing a long sleeveless tunic of blacks and grays. Belted at the waist, it bore a bixi (normally a length of cloth attached to the belt and flowing to a stop between the wearer's knees) made of azure fire.

"A Sheshish monk?" She couldn't hide her surprise... Made no effort to, in fact. "Why would a *T'lendak* Devil like you stand arrayed as a monk from the northern *deserts*?" While her first question had been only slightly more affected than mild curiosity, her next one, however, drew down into a low, dangerous alto tone, accompanied by a narrow-eyed glare of bitterest cold. "More importantly, what is it you want, here in my realm?"

Both boy and creature moved as one as they leered at her, expressions matching in disturbed mimicry.

"I knew I sensed the workings of a forge here!" Lanian's voice was childish triumph, as if he'd just been told he'd been given the last extra helping of pudding. "But you're only an acolyte..."

"Little fiend," Ylspeth began. "I neither know nor care what you're prattling about." Her voice was glacial, propelled by decades, lifetimes of nobility. "Before I separate you from the boy—"

"And what?" He laughed. "Send me back to the Hells? My dear acolyte, you have no idea with whom you—"

"Send you back to the Hells?" She filled the room with her own laughter, full of scorn and derision. "I won't be sending you anywhere. No, little fiend, I mean to craft something out of you. Shoes, perhaps a chamber pot... Something appropriately mundane." She lifted her right hand, fingers splayed, crackling silver energy arcing between them.

The T'lendak devil—the boy's keeper—began to twist in on itself. It doubled over as if suddenly afflicted with stomach pains.

As she walked forward, the boy dipped down for a moment, then leapt into the air. He rose impossibly high, nearly brushing his small head against the vaulted apex of the fifteen-foot ceiling. Before he came down, he landed six open palm strikes to Arafad's head, causing him to stagger. As he landed, Lanian took Arafad by his belt and right arm, maneuvering him as if he were a giant doll, and shoved him toward Ylspeth.

"Patternsmith..." Lanian hissed this with a venom that seemed profane coming out of a child's mouth.

Ylspeth dropped her hand at once. She had no interest in trying to separate Arafad from the creature that drove him. Doing so would make his body little more than a statue, and the power she'd employed would only work on a creature in direct line of sight. It couldn't burn through one target to strike the one behind it. Now that the T'lendak had moved, he would continue to do so, playing the child's game of the willow dance: circling around, always keeping an object between them.

Alright, little fiend, we'll try something else.

"Yaru!" said she. "Hold him!"

Yaru dropped his bow where he knelt, arrow still knocked to its string, and rose to obey.

"You won't have the chance to do that again, acolyte." Lanian's voice had been replaced utterly by the deep, guttural sound of his keeper. Once more he spoke the word acolyte with a knowing venom, as if he'd uncovered some misdeed, and were threatening to blackmail her with that knowledge. "Now that I'm certain of the power I sensed, it'll be a simple enough matter to track down the Forge. I'm afraid," he grinned, voice full of black joy, "...you're simply not needed anymore, *Your Excellency.*"

Ylspeth moved to sidestep the still-lumbering Arafad, but stopped herself in midcareer. He was glowing. She saw the spark of blue energy growing from within his core, expanding outward, filling his every limb like water being poured into an empty vessel.

"Catch me!" Lanian shouted, his voice once more that of a child.

She saw him turn and leap out of the window. She had just enough time to glance back at Arafad who bore an expression of pain and confusion that looked far too human on his face.

The blue energy expanded within him at a breakneck pace, brightening from blue to blinding white in the time it took her to register what Lanian's keeper had said.

"Mistress?"

Arafad's explosion turned the top floor into a silvery pyre. The heat was intense, but as the initial blast died away, Ylspeth still stood, singed but unbowed.

Still burning, she saw Yaru, his target now gone, pick up his bow and resume firing toward the eastern courtyard below. His body wouldn't last long. Already he was slowing, his head a torch above his shoulders.

She looked down at the full quiver still held in one hand. Bringing it back to her breast, cradling it the way she had the original piece of firewood, she drew in a deep breath of the burning air, closed her eyes, and waited. When she opened them again a moment later, she was no longer holding a quiver full of arrows. In her hand now rested a pristine crossbow, strung and ready to shoot.

She started to move, then stopped herself. Glaring down at the arrow in her other hand as if it had personally offended her, she gritted her teeth and hissed at it.

"Untether the fiend. Send him back to the hells from whence he came. with the taste of ashes to comfort him." Before her eyes, the arrow shrunk in length and thickened. Its steel head had become serrated, gleaming like newly polished silver.

Fitting the bolt in place, she stalked down the stairs to put an end to this.

-III-

Nineteen men and women knelt in the dust before the Westsong manor house that black night. Nineteen men and women received their laurels, then rose to do battle with a foe as old as cradle tales.

Fourteen of them survived. Of their original nineteen, Robis, Samik, Yaru, Arafad, and Lamwreigh would not sit in places of honor, not hear men laud their names and their great deeds. They would never rest upon comfortable chairs before the fire or out in the sun, telling their grandchildren of their glorious youth, or the night they stood to defend their Countess and the unsung small folk of a little village in the northwest of Thorion County from an impossible, implacable evil.

Thinking about it made Kaith sick. It made him feel useless. He had fought, had even commanded, and still, better men than he had fallen. He knew there was nothing he could have done for them, but he replayed the battle over and over again. He could think of little else. Whether awake or asleep, every note of that red symphony haunted him, though none more so than the loss of Robis.

Ylspeth rode up beside him along his left. She looked exhausted. He wondered, idly, if she'd slept at all.

"You were wrong, your Excellency," he said as she approached within earshot.

"Was I?" Ylspeth asked. Her voice suggested no surprise, nor did it give any hint that she might be affronted by his less than cordial greeting.

"We've set a breakneck pace for Ashacre, sleeping in shifts on the backs of carts or riding double, in the arms of other people mounted in military saddles." Kaith's voice sounded haggard, but he wasn't slurring his speech. He was bone tired, but his mind was working, right enough. "Everything that attacked us was either beheaded or burned, so there's no chance that anything stood back up and started to follow."

Ylspeth nodded, offering no argument or debate.

"Despite all of that, we have absolutely no idea what set that curse upon us, or initially made the dead forget to lie still." He paused, meeting her eyes, then looking away again toward the horizon. "So yes, you were wrong."

Ylspeth considered him in silence for a long moment, then nodded tentatively. Her face bore a look of bitter resignation.

Nodding again, more firmly this time, she finally spoke. "You're right, Sir Kaith." Her voice sounded hollow somehow. After a brief span during which her mind's eye replayed her encounter with Lanian, she added, "It most certainly is not over."

EPILOGUE

-I-

The manor house at Ashacre was, by comparison to the accommodations at Westsong, small and rather mean. The house itself had only one room with stone walls. Fortunately, that room was the Master's bedchamber. The rest of the building was made up of somewhat haphazard-looking additions of warped wooden wattles inconsistently (and inexpertly) sealed with random applications of daub. The result was a building that the wind and weather could sink their fangs into with relative ease.

The village was officially owned by the county itself. It was the sort of place that would likely be given to one of her knights upon his ascension to that lofty station, presuming they were not to be relegated to the status of bachelor-knight.

As she sat upon the featherbed in the modest stone chamber, Ylspeth realized she had to start considering what to do with her newly minted knights.

She had deliberately not declared The Nineteen to be elevated to the landed gentry, although that had been her ultimate intent for those who survived. A knight needed a manor if he were to maintain himself in a combat-ready state, after all. The income from such a settlement paid not only for that knight's daily bread, but for his household, his armsmen, and the maintenance of horses and gear of war so he could be called upon to serve at a moment's notice. It also fell to the knights to maintain order within and upon the lands over which he was given dominion.

She could hold to the letter of her word and grant the remaining fourteen their spurs as bachelors, she supposed. That would mean that the responsibility for their upkeep would fall to the sweat of their own brows, or the commissions the Thorion throne granted to them.

She toyed with this thought for a few idle moments, but she knew it wouldn't serve her purposes, nor would it be in keeping with her original intent. She needed them to remain loyal to her. Granting them title without the ability to sustain themselves would do little to engender their loyalty.

She turned her mind to the housekeeping aspects of what had come to pass. Eastshadow would need a new master, and she would need to summon the heir of Wick, Sir Reginald's eldest, and now only son, Ricgerd. The man was a lout, but as near as she could tell, he was quite loyal to the County Throne. He had his father's good nature, and his prowess with a blade, but wasn't possessed of many social graces.

It's as if Sirs Reginald and Anden had a child together. She laughed. The image was so absurd as she pictured the two men in various sexual positions that she couldn't help herself.

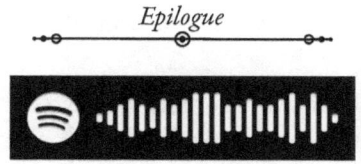

All too soon, however, the laughter had given way to sobs. Seeing Anden's face on the stage of her mind immediately brought thoughts of Valad. The tumble of memory and misery came on so suddenly, and with such ferocity, that her extraordinary self-possession winked out like a candle flame before a strong wind.

She drew her knees up to her chest, pressing her back against the cool stone wall. For a long moment, all she could do was try to weather the aching wave that rolled over her.

"Ylspeth..."

She closed her eyes more tightly as if the act would banish the voice.

"Ylspeth, come now. Look at me."

Shuddering, pinned between hope and terror, she lifted her face and opened her eyes. Through the wet prism of her tears, she saw him.

It wasn't Valad as he'd been days ago, however. No. This was Valad as he had been half a century up the hourglass. He'd been her companion, confidant, student, and teacher then. That had been a time before stone walls and wrought iron, when summer dozed all around them ... when the world was full of river-song and sun-dappled glens, and ascension to the throne was a lone, gray storm cloud against the otherwise endless blue.

He was once again young and beautiful, wearing what she had chidingly referred to as his Summer Costume— naked to the waist, every muscle on display, his brown waves longer, softer, begging her fingers to slide through them as she'd always longed to.

"Why did you leave me?" Her voice was a ragged whisper.

She hadn't meant to speak—hadn't meant to acknowledge this phantom's presence, but she found that she couldn't keep silent. The words had passed her lips before she'd had time to stop herself.

"I would never leave you. Surely you know that." His tone was as she remembered it—summer thunder mixed with pine song.

"And to Anden?" It was as if he hadn't spoken at all. "You could've bested that lout with a dagger between your teeth and both hands behind your back for good measure!" She kept her voice low so as not to unintentionally call Greggor or Valgar from the next room, but she was both angry and hurt.

"Any man can fall in battle. You know that." He paused for a moment as if considering, then continued, "And treachery and dishonor our deadlier weapons than any made of metal and wood."

She rose in anger, a white, burning emptiness that wanted to devour everything—anything in its path to fill that void.

"How dare you!" She crossed the three feet that stood between them in a single stride, balled up her fist, and struck him in the chest with it. Over, and over again she struck him. She felt the flesh and the taut muscle beneath clench and flex to absorb the blows as they came in, but otherwise, her assault was proving useless and ineffectual.

At length, elbows bent, forearms and balled fists pressed against his chest, she bowed her head. She pressed her brow to the warmth of his skin and remained there, a study in silent misery and mute acceptance.

"Better?"

She nodded, the tracks of her tears almost invisible in the bitter, salt and silver moonlight that fell through the rooms high and only window.

"I'm glad," said he.

For a span that may have lasted seconds or centuries, they simply stood. She could feel the moment rushing toward them and silently pleaded with herself to turn aside from it. Ignorance is the sweetest wine that ever was, after all, though it's rarely appreciated until it's been stripped away. She felt the end enfold her like frostbite—frigid until the last, when all is warmth and soft acceptance.

"Command me, Ylspeth. Tell me how I can serve you best." He was smiling. She could hear it in his voice, though her eyes remained closed, her brow still pressed to the warm silk of his chest. It hurt her heart to hear him speak so. "Tell me what you'd have of me. Tell me..." He paused for just a beat. "...Tell me how I can make you happy."

Silence pervaded the room for a pregnant, seemingly endless interval during which neither of them breathed.

"You can't." Her voice was steady again, under control once more. "You can't because you're gone. If you lived and were wounded only, if you hadn't been so damned stubborn and I hadn't been so indulgent, you'd have been here, waiting to talk to me right now. I'd have been able to fix you—to mend your broken body with you still inside of it. If it'd proven too much for me, then..."

In her mind's eye, she saw the handsome pair of children she had made for them. The boy, sturdy and broad-shouldered, had Valad's soft brown waves and her wise, mountain-top-blue eyes. The girl, broad-shouldered but nimble, had eyes that matched Valad's golden-flecked-brown. Her hair shone the honey color Ylspeth had worn in her youth.

"I would get to meet you again for the first time, watch you grow, and grow beside you if you'd agreed... If you'd only stayed a little longer, we could have had—" She chuckled, pulling her arms around him in a brief, tight embrace. "...forever."

She released him, pulling back and looking up into his handsome face.

"But I waited too long, didn't I?" She shook her head and stepped back. "Stood before me is nothing more than an echo of my oldest friend, perhaps my only friend. And while I'm grateful for this," she gestured down the length of his body with her left hand. "This moment, I know that I pulled you from my memory, that my grieving mind tapped into the power of the Forge and called you forth to try and find some semblance of comfort... To help me make sense of it, and to say..." She drew in a ragged breath, then a second before she felt she had the strength to finish it. "...To say good ... goodbye."

He nodded, straightening his back and clasping his hands behind it. He still bore a smile, but now it was tinged with a mixture of sadness and resigned acceptance.

"...And you no longer need ... the illusion?"

She smiled, a few last tears sliding down the soft curves of her face.

"No. I no longer need the illusion."

"If you should ever find that you do... If you should ever require my counsel, my shoulder again, you have but to call. I meant what I said, Ylspeth. I will never leave you."

She squeezed her eyes shut. Drawing a last breath, she pulled it down past her navel and held it for a long moment. When she opened her eyes again, she was alone.

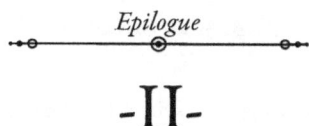

-II-

Just after dawn, Greggor knocked at, then opened, her chamber door. There were neither slaves nor servants in residence, so he himself carried the small bowl of thin stew which would have to serve as her breakfast. She ate without much relish, but with a fixed and focused intent. She didn't much care for the trappings of public life which required her to eat and drink in front of others, but she'd become reluctantly accustomed to it.

As she ate, Greggor, ever the efficient administrator, detailed in brief all the preparations and respective statuses of their wagons, horse and oxen teams, her knights, and the dozen peasants that had fled Westsong with them. When he'd finished, and was rising to take away the remnants of her meal, she held him fast with a question.

"Sir Greggor, have you given much thought in the last few hours as to your future service to the Thorion Throne?"

"I have, Excellency." Greggor's voice was uncharacteristically tentative. "But I fear I haven't come to any useful conclusions."

"It is certainly within your right, and one could even argue that it is your duty, to maintain control over a manorial estate, in order to support yourself as a knight of this realm."

"Aye." His face fell rather comically. "Yet, as you know, knighthood was never something I actively sought. I've always been quite content to serve the throne—to serve *you* in the same capacity I have for so many years."

She nodded, looked thoughtful for a moment, then changed the subject rather abruptly.

"Apart from your good self, who would you select from among your fellows yesterday as an effective leader?"

He paused for only a brief span before answering. "Barnic, Kaith, Marcza, and Valgar."

"Anyone else?"

"No, Excellency. The others, to a man, are stalwart and effective on the field. They're good folk as well, which is important. Loyal folk."

"But none of them displayed leadership beyond those four." He shook his head. As always, he was unapologetic for delivering plain truth without embellishment. Facts were facts. While there was no need to be crude or harsh, Greggor had never, in her experience at least, elected to dress facts in finery.

"Out of them, who would you say had the most tactical and strategic sense of the battlefield?"

"All of them had a fair tactical sense of the field, but if we are attempting to winnow down candidates, I would remove Barnic from the list. His instincts and tactical ability are excellent, but quite reactionary."

"...And strategy?"

"If we're speaking of adhering to the strategic goals set before them, all three are capable. If we're speaking of determining strategy – developing it... Now we must eliminate Valgar. He understands the battlefield quite well. He can easily hold on to a long-term strategy. However, he's unlikely to suggest one on his own. Valgar's creative within the box he's put in, but not quite creative enough to go and build a box himself."

"That leaves us with Sir Kaith and Dame Marcza."

Greggor nodded a single time. He put on a thoughtful expression which lasted an uncharacteristically long time compared to his usual air of quiet competence.

"Excellency," he said at last. "What, if I may, do you expect Kaith or Marcza to organize and lead?" He followed this question almost immediately with, "If I overstepped by asking…"

"Not at all," Ylspeth said, smiling genuinely for what felt like the first time in weeks. "What happened at Westsong was not, unless I am very much mistaken, an isolated incident. It was the first stroke in a larger war." She nodded at the man's widening eyes, the closest thing Greggor ever got to a look of shock. "Yes, I said war. Moreover, it will be a war the likes of which the wider world, to say nothing of County Thorion, is currently woefully unprepared to survive, let alone win."

"So the order you intend to have one of these two lead is your first step in readying, at the least, County Thorion to weather the storm?"

She nodded. Inwardly, she thanked all the gods that ever were that Greggor had survived to ride out of Westsong with her.

"As much as I would love to tell you that Kaith is the best choice…"

"You don't think that he is." She nodded, then asked the obvious question. "Why not?"

"She has more skill with the sword, more word fame even before the events of Westsong, is the scion of a respected member of the gentry, and she is the only one of the pair who lost blood kin at Westsong."

"I note you did not say that she was a better strategist or leader then Sir Kaith."

"She isn't, nor is Kaith better in those areas than she. If those were our only concerns when selecting a potential leader, the decision would be difficult."

Ylspeth adopted the ghost of a grin and nodded.

"She'll keep them talking, if only to criticize the fact that a woman has been put in charge of an important military order. Should it become necessary, she will almost certainly defeat those who press that particular point too firmly in court—either by virtue of her sharp tongue or her sword-arm. Overall, she will serve to rally peasant and noble alike to whatever banner—whatever cause or duty you assign her."

"Go on, Sir Greggor. Say it."

"Aye, as you say, Excellency." He drew in a single breath, held it for a moment, then did as he'd been bidden. "Dame Marcza will be able to lead men into battle and back out again in victory. Her hard-won respect and unmistakable prowess will see to that. Moreover, she will draw people to her. Could our Kaith inspire others? I think we both know the answer to that, if I may make so bold a claim. Yes, he certainly could, can, and ultimately will. Dame Marcza, however, already does. She inspires..."

"Peace, Greggor. I agree with you completely."

Greggor nodded.

"I will think of an appropriate thing to call this new order as we ride back to the capital, but its purpose is twofold. The first is to prepare both its own members, and the rest of the county's chivalry and soldiery, for the coming war. The second, arguably more important, is to create unity among those same folk."

Greggor nodded and smiled. Both that smile and his next words augured well for Ylspeth's plan for his future.

"Tournament season is at an end," said he. "Now we train for war."

Nodding, she stood and walked toward the door. Opening it, she cast her conspirator's eye around the outer hall and toward the common room. No one stood close enough to be of any concern. Ducking her head back into the room, she shut the door and walked back toward where Greggor still stood.

"Sir Greggor, I hereby grant to you the manor and holdings of Knell's Stone."

"Excellency..." For a moment all he could do was gape.

"You will need that particular place to be under your control as we go forward."

At last, he'd recovered enough to speak. His mind was working once more.

"But surely one of Sir Val—"

"Be silent," said she, resuming her seat. Her voice was gentle, but the look in her eyes drew him up short. "I must tell, must *trust* someone now that he is gone. It's only fitting that someone be you. He selected you for my retinue himself. Did you know that?" Greggor looked thunderstruck. "Well, never mind. We need to discuss a great many things over the course of the next several days. You cannot help me or the County against this threat if I do not rightly arm you with the information you need."

Greggor managed to accept this with the majority of his customary air of professionalism still firmly intact. Still, there was a tiny light burning behind each of his eyes.

Greggor had thought he'd known all of her Excellency's—most of the county's—secrets. To discover that there was yet more he didn't know, and that he was to be given access to it? In Sir Greggor's mind, no chest of gold or grant of land could equal such a gift.

There are three things that I must do. I must empower Dame Marcza to unify both chivalry and soldiery, I must teach Greggor about the Forge and tell him what I suspect about the T'lendak that possessed Lanian, and I must investigate, and either ally with or subjugate this land to the north—this Dereek khn. If, as it seems, they defeated the lady of the Shivering Song...

"For now..." Ylspeth turned her mind away from the grander strategy she saw before her to focus on the tactics that would support it. "Please send Dame Marcza to me."

Greggor nodded, bowed, and moved toward the door. Just before he opened it, he turned his head back to face her.

"Your Excellency..." He turned his body so that he faced her fully once again. "He was a great man. I can never take his place, but please know that I will do whatever I can to fill his shoes."

She bowed her head. "Thank you." Her voice was little more than a whisper. Before she'd raised her chin again, he had already taken his soundless leave.

Rising from her perch on the bed, Ylspeth embraced a bitter truth. For the first time in years beyond count, she was truly afraid. Oh, there had been moments of panic, but in all the years since they'd first found the Forge, she had never really been afraid. Well, fear be damned. Thorion County belonged to her. No nightmare, living or dead, would change that.

She heard hollow, hard, knocking sounds as boots strode down the hall toward her chamber. A moment later, Dame Marcza's voice floated in past the closed door.

"Excellency? You wanted to speak with me?"

...And so it begins.

In accordance with rite and tradition, the Thorion Throne does hereby forge a new chivalric order. Its robe and office: to protect the lives of Thorion's people and their allies from any and all forces that threaten to extinguish their light.

Hear now the tenets of the order: to teach and to train, to listen and to learn, to speak and to sponsor, to fight and to forgive, to dream and to die in service to this worthy charge.

With these words, The Thorion Throne does hereby ordain and establish The Order of The Valadin, and names Dame Mareza of Southwall as its Commander.

Done this day, 38 Gerstesykli, Thorionin vuosi 481.

Countess Elspeth of Thorion
Sir Robis of Wick
Dame Mareza of Southwall
Sir Greggor of Frostfecht
Sir Valgar of Burchorg
Sir Alnik of Westsong
Sir Taran of Coille Sàmhach
Sir Lamwreigh of Eastshadow
Sir Larn of The Last Grass
Sir Arafad of The Last Grass

Sir Barnie of Knell's Stone
Sir Lastar of Knell's Stone
Sir Aethan of Knell's Stone
Sir Raegus of Knell's Stone
Sir Gordan of Knell's Stone
Sir Hemmet of Southwall
Sir Rann of Southwall
Sir Samik of Stone's Pond
Sir Edren of Oakwind
Sir Kaith of Thorion

These nineteen men and women knelt in the dust before the Red Storm at Westsong, then rose to do battle with a foe as old as cradle tales. May the echo of their valor and loyalty outlast the knell of Havoc's Horn, and linger until the stars refuse to shine.

The Drums of Unrest, The Next Installment of The Cycle of Bones series Coming Soon!

ACKNOWLEDGEMENTS

There are many, many people without whom I could not have written and released this book, and all of the books that will follow in The Cycle of Bones, and future series.

Jim Trice, Dawn Hart, David Shepherd, Diane Worden, Ed & Scott Abbot, Sean Dorosinski, and Knut Martin Fjelldal: You made up the foundation upon which I stood, and without which this Novella would never have come to pass.

My Beta readers on this project: Katey (Mak), Chris (Dawg), Owen (Road) and, of course, my editorial staff Lauren and Gwen, your individual and collective help was (as always) invaluable and insightful.

Jeff Brown—the man responsible for bringing the faces and places in my head to startling and stunning life; my only complaint is having to wait until the next book is ready for art before I get to work with you again.

To my Hastati Gard—it was an honor and one of the great joys of my life to train, stand, and fight at your side. Protego Regnum.

A special and enormous thank you to my Patrons on Patreon. Your love and support makes all of this madness possible in more ways than just the obvious financial one.

Lastly; a thank you to Corwyn's Cadre. You've been with me for years as I recorded and toured, fought and foundered, and you've proven not just willing, but excited to walk down this new road at my side. You continue to humble me. I hope to always make you proud.

Thanks for all the Electricity,
JP Corwyn

Author's Note

...And now you know where it all started.

Hey Cadre! It's excellent to see all of you again. Yes, yes, in a turn of events shocking to absolutely nobody, we've kicked things off with a blind joke.

Now, bear with me while I catch up your new brothers and sisters on what they've missed. Grab a cuppa or something. I'll get back with you in half-a-mo.

To you, then, new reader, welcome home. Let me see if I can't catch you up on a few things.

I'm JP Corwyn - your Friendly Neighbourhood Blind Guy. I'm a legally blind singer, songwriter, composer, and (obviously) Military Fantasy/Horror author.

This book - The Dawn of Unions - was my debut.

I originally released it (as well as The Drums of Unrest and The Eaters of Time,) as an independent author. While I was working on the next volume in The Cycle of Bones (that'd be *The Echo of Tombs*) a chance meeting brought the endearing and indomitable Erika Lance and me into contact with one another. And *that* ultimately led to my signing with her publishing house: 4HP.

As a part of the publishing deal, we agreed to rerelease the extant three books with the rest of the series to follow. It was also decided that *Dawn* would be marked (quite rightly) as a prequel for the rerelease - a *Book 0*.

This was exciting for a number of reasons—not least because it gave me the chance to re-edit and revise the books before re-release. Predictably there were a few warts, as it were, discovered after publication. Nothing I couldn't *live with*, but there were a few things I didn't want my *readers* to have to endure unnecessarily.

As the legendary Simon Vance was kind enough to point out to me, mistakes are normal for even the most well-known and successful authors.

As a side note, I can't help but grin as I realize he'll be reading this for the audiobook revision, but I calls it like I sees it. Yep—another blind joke. You'll get used to that.

In any event, while I was pleased to go through the editorial process for *Drums* and *Eaters* as if they were brand new manuscripts, it was important to me to leave *this* book relatively unscathed. It's gone through a final quality control edit, of course, and there were a *few* sections that I couldn't leave untouched (for example: one of the verses for Silver in the Skies actually went out with an older version in the original print run, meaning the soundtrack didn't match the printed word), it was important to me that my earliest published work was left largely intact. I think it's important to be able to see where things truly began and how they've progressed. To that end, QC notwithstanding, I wanted readers to see the book *warts and all,* as they say.

Had *Dawn* gone through a full revision, the story would've been the same, but the writing itself would've changed. I am, or so I'm led to believe, a far better writer now that I'm half a million words into The Cycle of Bones than I was when I began it.

So, here we are! Okay Cadre, they're caught up. Now for the rest of the story, so to speak.

Those who came to this book already aware of who I am and what I'm about came *away* from it with the same shared thought.

"All right Blind Guy, we *know* those are real songs. You're *you*. Of *course,* they're real songs. So... where and when can we hear them?"

A fair question.

The soundtrack for *Dawn* is available online kinda ... everywhere. Those of you who're holding the print version of this book will have noticed QR codes on a few key pages. Those codes, if scanned, will take you directly to the Spotify page where that song can be found. Alternatively, the songs are up on most music streaming platforms and are available on my YouTube channel, along with the *Scions of Skolf* animated series—a brief history of the world in which the books take place.

I've got soundtracks in the works for each book in the series in varying states of completion. Music is, after all, a large part of who I am, and this seemed like an excellent way to merge my two worlds.

After the re-releases are sorted, future installments in The Cycle of Bones will be released at least once a year until the series is finished. Counting this book, I have ten volumes planned in this series. It may be that it winds up compressed to nine or expanded to as many as twelve, but ten is the current plan.

As for what's to come? Now that Ylspeth, Kaith, and the others have weathered The Red Storm at Westsong, I think it's fair to say that Ylspeth had the right of it.

"...And so it begins."

~JP Corwyn
Coral Springs, FL/Newmarket, UK
2023

Book Club Questions

1. Kaith was clearly the protagonist of the story, but was he its hero? If not, who was?

2. In antiquity, serfs were not property in the way slaves were. Yet they had severe limitations on their rights and freedoms, so were not strictly free. Before the battle began, Ylspeth knighted Westsong's remaining trained fighters, and made free men and women out of its citizens. Why did she take this step? What purpose did it serve?

3. Before losing too much vision to allow him to continue, the author spent more than a decade fighting and training others to fight in unchoreographed, armored melee combat. Corwyn sought to bring that experience to his writing... to give access to a side of battle that leaves readers feeling as if they'd been in a battle, rather than just witnessing one from a safe distance. Was this successful? Did you feel as if you were there in the shield wall at Westsong, or that you'd seen or read about the battle?

4. Should Sir Valad have killed Sir Anden? How might that have changed the events of the story beyond that point?

5. Kaith clearly suffers from bouts of imposter syndrome. Has he, in your opinion, truly earned his spurs? Is he worthy of the rank of knighthood, or is he right to feel like an imposter?

6. Clearly Ylspeth feels that she did what was necessary at Westsong. She takes a longer view of events than most would. While she doesn't take pleasure in throwing lives away, she's absolutely willing to do so in service to her larger goals. Is she right to view things through such a long-term lens, or has that practice made her too aloof?

7. In Lamwreigh's final conversation with Lanian, did you—even for a moment—believe that Lamwreigh had actually gotten through to his younger brother?

Author Bio

How could you be so blind? You haven't heard of JP Corwyn? ...Haven't seen him live? ...Haven't heard his music? How embarrassing for you!

It's okay. You're in the right place. For JP, the rationale for the blind jokes is, well, reasonable. He is legally blind. Born with a degenerative eye condition; his genre tags of Blind Indie Rock, and now Blind Indie Prose make more sense. Otherwise, he'd just be sort of pretentious and snarky, but not in the fun depraved sit-com way.

Corwyn's vocal-driven indie rock style is infectious, described as "Shinedown and Angie Aparo on a tour bus... With Stevie Wonder driving!" On vocals and acoustic guitar, Corwyn has helmed an EP, four full-length albums, and numerous single releases thus far in his career. He has taken a raw, and unplugged show from Tampa, up the east coast to New York, overseas to the UK, EU, and Asia, and back again.

...But Corwyn's harbored a dark, secret obsession throughout his musical career: his other driving force—writing fiction. Corwyn started work on "The Cycle of Bones" in early 2019. This epic multi-book series burned its way onto the literary scene with the novella "The Dawn of Unions" (November 2019). It has continued with the novels "The Drums of Unrest" (November 2020) and "The Eaters of Time" (September 2022). Combining his passions, JP has recorded soundtracks for the first two books, including an original cinematic score and songs appearing in the pages of the novels.

Yep, he's blind. But he's hardly unaware. So why should you be?

MORE BOOKS FROM
4 HORSEMEN PUBLICATIONS

HORROR, THRILLER, & SUSPENSE

ALAN BERKSHIRE
Jungle
Hell's Road

ERIKA LANCE
Jimmy
Illusions of Happiness
No Place for Happiness
I Hunt You

MARIA DEVIVO
Witch of the Black Circle
Witch of the Red Thorn
Witch of the Silver Locust

MARK TARRANT
The Mighty Hook

STEVE ALTIER
The Ghost Hunter

FANTASY

D. LAMBERT
To Walk into the Sands
Rydan
Celebrant
Northlander
Esparan
King
Traitor
His Last Name

DANIELLE ORSINO
Locked Out of Heaven
Thine Eyes of Mercy
From the Ashes
Kingdom Come
Fire, Ice, Acid, & Heart
A Fae is Done

J.M. PAQUETTE
Klauden's Ring
Solyn's Body
The Inbetween
Hannah's Heart

LOU KEMP
The Violins Played
Before Junstan
Music Shall Untune the Sky
The Raven and the Pig
The Pirate Danced and the
Automat Died
The Sea of the Vanities

R.J. YOUNG
Challenges of Tawa
The Witch of the Whirlwind

SYDNEY WILDER
Daughter of Serpents

VALERIE WILLIS
Cedric: The Demonic Knight
Romasanta: Father of
Werewolves

The Oracle: Keeper of the
Gaea's Gate
Artemis: Eye of Gaea
King Incubus: A New Reign

KYLE SORRELL
Munderworld
Potarium

**DISCOVER MORE AT
4HORSEMENPUBLICATIONS.COM**